Paper Trail

ARLEEN PARÉ

NEWEST PRESS

Library and Archives Canada Cataloguing in Publication
Paré, Arleen, 1946-
Paper trail / Arleen Paré.

(Nunatak fiction)
ISBN-13: 978-1-897126-13-4
ISBN-10: 1-897126-13-1

I. Title. II. Series.

PS8631.A7425P36 2007   C813'.6   C2006-906626-4

Editor for the press: Suzette Mayr
Cover and interior design: Katherine Melnyk
Author Photo: Chris Fox

NeWest Press acknowledges the support of the Canada Council for the Arts and the Alberta Foundation for the Arts, and the Edmonton Arts Council for our publishing program. We also acknowledge the financial support of the Government of Canada through the Book Publishing Industry Development Program (BPIDP) for our publishing activities.

NeWest Press
201–8540–109 Street
Edmonton, Alberta T6G 1E6
(780) 432-9427
www.newestpress.com

NeWest Press is committed to protecting the environment and to the responsible use of natural resources. This book is printed on 100% post-consumer recycled and ancient-forest-friendly paper. For more information, please visit www.oldgrowthfree.com.

PRINTED AND BOUND IN CANADA
1 2 3 4 5 10 09 08 07

For Chris Fox, loving companion through the bureaucratic years, and beyond; and for those workers in government-funded bureaucracies everywhere who, despite the inherent difficulties of their positions, try hard to provide good service to the public.

ACKNOWLEDGEMENTS

Infinite and heartfelt gratitude to: Betsy Warland, for setting me on course and seeing me through; Mary Schendlinger, for encouraging me to submit earlier parts of this work to *Geist* magazine; Smaro Kamboureli, for looking at the manuscript when it needed to be looked at; Suzette Mayr, for editing so skillfully, patiently, and thoroughly; Chris Fox, for encouraging me and being an invaluable and sensitive first reader.

What I know is this. I'm giving up. No offense. I was never committed. Not ever, to offices.

From *Land to Light On* by Dionne Brand

And I have seen dust from the walls of institutions,
Finer than flour, alive, more dangerous than silica,
Sift, almost invisible, through long afternoons of tedium

From "Dolor" by Theodore Roethke

the heart is not a door, but it opens

From *In Cannon Cave* by Carole Glasser Langille

Frances grumbled out of nightmares early Monday morning, rolled over and found a finger by her ear. She forced her head off the pillow and watched as the small digit slid into the cotton dip where her head had been. She reached up, careful not to disturb the pillow and switched on the reading light over the bed. Pink as a piglet, it lay curved with a wrinkled knuckle and a maroon-polished scallop of nail at the tip. It rested on the white pillow case, clean and bloodless, as though galleried. She pulled her hands to eye level and wiggled her fingers. The baby finger was missing from her left hand. Good Lord, she thought, I have that meeting with Finance today, I don't have time to deal with this. She flicked off the reading light and sank back down as her clock radio blared its 6 AM invasion. But first (the announcer sounded pleased) Our headlines: More military success in the Middle East; the Canadian dollar is up slightly from yesterday's low; Ottawa promises lower taxes for corporations.

At least the finger was her own. She scooped it from her pillow and folded it into the palm of her right hand, as light as a dead caterpillar.

My job's too much. Her left leg twitched. How can I lie in bed like this? A headache edged in from behind her right ear. I'm losing my waistline, my teeth are falling out, and now this!

She stared at the ceiling, a pale horizon, and kneaded her left shoulder. The radio told her that twenty-four people had been turned away from city shelters overnight. She yanked back the covers with her free hand, careful not to squash the finger in the other, and swung her feet onto the carpet.

The baby finger fit into her jewellery box beside the two molars from the previous week. All three body parts snuggled together in the tiny black compartment, separated from the earrings and the lapel pins by thin velvet-covered dividers. Twenty-one similar compartments surrounded a larger central area where Frances kept her bracelets and rings, hair elastics and spare business cards. Some of the smaller compartments were empty. Room for a few more parts, she thought, if life was going to be this way.

It wasn't even 6:15. She jerked open the top drawer of the tallboy, pulled out a bra, underpants, pantyhose, and a slip the colour of old newsprint. The latest colour, the woman in lingerie had told her. She bought the slip anyway; it had the advantage of fitting her and these days, with her added pounds, she felt grateful for its generous waist and drape. None of the red slips came in her new size. She couldn't really see the colour this morning; next door's backyard spotlight filtered only half-light through her window shades.

When she switched on the dresser lamp, pools of yellow surrounded uneven stacks. Papers and books jumbled on top of the dresser. They spread on the carpet beside her bed. She kicked the largest book under the bed. Shoot. That's twice now, she thought. It hurt her last night too. After she reviewed the latest contracts for the Good Will Works Society, she cracked open Shelters in American Inner Cities: The Case Against. When she woke up in the middle of the night the book lay aslant on her forehead, one hard corner jammed into her skin. She rubbed the dent on her cheek and then didn't get back to sleep until four, maybe later; the last time she looked at the LED, it blued 3:58.

On her Queen Anne chair, yesterday's grey sweater peeked out from under last week's management report. On the floor, her black patent shoes balanced on a stack of policy binders. Her eyes drifted to the desk where Lieder Music From Days Gone By lay open. She flipped to her favorite song, Mahler's "Oft denk' ich, sie sind nur ausgegangen!", cleared her throat once, twice, and then sang the tune through, intoning the last line a second time in a clear, sombre contralto: it is a beautiful day on those heights, it is a beautiful day on those heights. She sang it through again in the shower. Her headache floated from the right to the left side of her head.

Very late now, she pulled on the navy suit she'd worn the day before yesterday, pairing it with an emerald green sweater she found in a dry cleaner's bag at the back of the closet. She pushed gold hoops through the holes in her ears and noticed that her earlobes felt loose. She tugged at her earlobes, and in the mirror watched her mouth open.

She pursed her lips and shoved her arms through the sleeves of the navy blue jacket. Its pinstripes were emerald green.

Before she left her bedroom, she yanked the roller blind. It whipped up with the clatter of wooden spoons and flipped itself twice around the roller bar. The sky's opalescence was beginning to drown the glare of the spotlight next door. They never turned it off.

Halfway down the stairs, she remembered it was Monday. She really should phone Gregor; it was their arrangement: Monday and Wednesday mornings. But she was so *late now and she knew her husband would be too busy to notice whether or not it was Monday or Wednesday or any other day for that matter. His research in New Mexico was going well, he had told her on Wednesday when they last spoke. He'd be home in a couple of months.*

I fixed you some tea, dear, her mother called as Frances hit the last step.

I don't have time.

And a bran muffin.

Her mother followed Frances with the hot mug and the muffin, one in each hand, to the front door. Here, she said. Frances had her coat on and her gloves. The left glove's baby finger hung limp. She hefted her bulging briefcase. In her other hand she held her car keys and her scarf. She waited for her mother to open the door.

No offense, dear, her mother said, placing the muffin on the cabinet under the mirror, but that caterwauling this morning was frightful. Your father thought you were having a seizure. We're not ungrateful for your hospitality, Frances dear, but really. She stepped out of her mules, holding the tea in front of her. We love staying here. She jammed one foot, then the other, into her high-heeled boots, and left the zips undone.

I'll take these out to the car for you.

Not the muffin, said Frances.

＊　＊　＊

I fall through middle night and chronologic files of buckled sleep
                                        while printed pages wheel
                    wide and numbers sift like urban soot.
Another meeting ticks the fingers of my minute hand. My eyes grey
                    boardroom walls, and sudden stacks of hat-high papers
                            slip, then slide. From lips, from table's maple edge,
            collapsing folders, high-rise of cards.

That diurnal sleight, colliding nighttime
                    into day while still the sequenced memos fall and flip,
fade in, fade out, whirl white. Sharp-edged, they bite and slice
                                        before they silt the floor.
Click: if . . . time,
            then . . . money. If Monday,
                                    then mourning coils
            somewhere near the surface, rises.
                                        I tuck sheets
        around my dawning head. If drowning. Edges me
        toward the lip. Losing threads.

    The room begins to panic, tip. My eyes refuse.

The room filling with half-light. Insists. Half-light: unnerving as a single
bulb dangling one hundred watts from a single
                        length of cord. Monday morning slips
                                        like broken ice. Slips
                                            another five.

Part One
LINEAR EQUATIONS

When I go I will not remember these years. The way a woman might not recall the pain of childbirth. The pain falls away.

Countdown: Equals 206 days. Actual working. Days to go. Tomorrow 205.

When I go I will not look back. No pillars of salt.
This is about time and money and counting.   Serious.

Even now counting down.
Ticking off each calendar day.

About work, which is only for
the fittest, which in me is only partial. I am only partially fit. Parts of me in secret. Sitting on a chain-link fence. Thinking about my Swiss Army watch. Thinking about my bank account. Thinking about the chain-link fence. How it swings.

This is the final year. Making like I'm fitting in. Fitful. Fistfuls in the bank. Safe as. Houses on the ground. As though.

And about you, Kafka   because your name signifies this place
sanctifies this understanding
    you were with us once
        among the papers and the records and the bureaucratic ruins
    refusing not to say
  scribe of fears   of corridors   I now inhabit

unable to maintain my own not saying I say your name: invocation and plea
knowing once I saw you   Kafka
    saw your dark blue back rushing down a hall   skidding round a corner
disappearing through an unseen door
And I called: *stop!*   the word leaping from my unfit mouth   collapsing
down the hall like a tipsy stack of memos

I phoned you later (having dreamed the number). Left the message. I need
to know: how did you write this once. Mine is much the same: offices
are offices, squared with desks confined and drowning; bureaucracy is
bureaucracy, passive in the voice. Officialdom is power and grey by any
other name is grey. Who measures its literary value?   You understood the
lifetime weight of office work, the ache between the shoulders, the way a
face drifts blank.

Call me at my office, help me with this leaving, my escape, help me write
me out.

Even now I'm counting down.

Let this stand as my attempt
to record my time
wandering in this officious bewilderness.
My belly full of days.

I strap on my watch before I leave the house each morning the way a cowboy straps on a pistol, a diver oxygen. Tools of. Time is what I trade.

I strap myself into that time–money equation. They pay a lot of money for my time. Vacation pay and benefits, dental, medical, extended. No sheriff comes to get me in the morning, no boss drags me out of bed, throws me in my car. My eyes are wide. I sign myself in. Load my own gun. Set my own alarm clock. Pack my own briefcase. It's what I know. It's called free will. You'd think I would be happy.

I trade it in, time, and it peels off, one by one. Day after tomorrow, 204.

he said my mother never worked

for money   that she never had a job

he handed her the dollar bills
        for milk and tea and cans of crushed tomatoes
        she walked
        in winter took the bus
        the shopping mall   2 miles away
she banked the change from discounts specials on the crushed tomatoes
        money for her work
                around his house
        to fry his steaks
        shovel his driveway
        take his temper
she kept her own account

their contract unspoken
like all the others on our block

How my father would say: As the twig is bent, so grows the tree. Pliable and bent. Like me.

If something's worth doing, it's worth doing well. Workaholic and spent. Like him.

How elocution lessons were so important. That he took elocution when he was thirteen, his last year of schooling. He stood in the kitchen in his black business shoes, his mouth a perfect O articulating the second syllable of the word el-O-cution, his eyes steady on me. Asked if I ever got elocution in school. I only knew to tell him no. The strangeness of that word: elocution, like electric shock or electric chair or execution; electrocution, part elephant, part locomotion. He said it made all the difference, those lessons, when he turned thirteen, in elocution.

How he wished he'd gone into politics. Ever think of it? he'd ask, of going into politics . . . or medicine? How, though he asked me, I knew he meant him. No chance for him, leaving school so young. Working at anything until he came to America. Then working and working. At anything. Making sinks for Crane Inc., when he didn't know a thing about them. Driving a horse-drawn bakery truck door-to-door in Montreal ice storms, the old brown horse skidding down the icy streets, falling down the hills.

Selling soap. Selling machines. Selling dances. Selling wax. Selling. Anything. He said.

she could not tell him the true cost of things
          not tell him when she bought her new blue dress, or
when we needed shoes or when the price of canned tomatoes rose 3 cents.
not tell him anything.

the price she paid. Inside the house with the electric range, the chesterfield
washer-dryer, her packs of Rothmans, the wall-to-walls, the budgie bird.

some days arriving home from school we said:
          you were napping.
no, she said. emphatic. pillow creases on her cheek.

she never minded lying. it never hurt her heart. it was just another price.

housework was not work, it was her everyday:
she painted the living room; mowed the grass; dusted
the Royal Doulton figurines; knit us Mary Maxim sweaters;
baked pineapple upside-down cake; reupholstered the fraying footstool.
everyday she made our beds. after we had laid in them.

My mother did not sufficiently socialize me, train me to work, inside or outside, especially outside the house. (Blame it on my mother.)

Not deeply. Not enough. (Blame it on *I Love Lucy*.)

Later, I figured out the inside: Clean floors before your feet stick to them, wash dishes to eat off the next day, take out the garbage when it's full. It makes domestic sense. The logic of the outside I have not learned. Sufficiently. Except it comes with rewards. Like paycheques. The rest is strictly surreal, between the covers of Kafka's books, requiring acts of faith, or applications of irony.

My father
    At the kitchen table, chrome, red vinyl top.
    With his cup of milky tea   two sugars   first cigarette wafting by his cup.
    Legs crossed   red vinyl chair pushed back half a foot.
                Leaning in to meet his cup halfway.
                Making that sound.

Every morning.   This morning
                in his grey silk suit.
                The man   my father
leaves the house, wins the bread.   Eats bitter
marmalade and Salada tea with Export A's. Wears
black buffed shoes and new-bought business suits.
The more he leaves the house the more he can't get back.

                My mother
                in her housedress flowered beige and pink two
                buttons missing down the front leaning elbows
                on her kitchen counter out the window watching
                weather dishes in the sink her mug of instant
                coffee her call-in radio show Wondertoast with
                jam and peanut butter. The more she stays at
                home the more she can't get out.

For the record, I begin the night before:

Begin at 10 when I check the alarm is set, thinking morning meeting with the finance team, thinking what to wear. Or begin at 3, when I wake to hiss of rain, roll over, tuck my pillow round my ear, listen to my brain talking to itself, planning what to say to finance. Or at 6, when the radio cracks sleep's thin shell, announcing: economy in trouble, interests rates up, rain today. All day.

These are only times when cracks appear, when I imagine I can insert beginning. Make like there's a storyline of work that unravels out of early mornings, meetings every day and memos, e-mails, office windows, desks and drawers and Anacin at 4.

At 6:01 I roll over like a river log. Turn off the radio. Fold into arms that open in her sleep. Her Hollywood eye-shades rest askew, honey hair pushed up and over the elastic on one side. She lies all breast-soft and warm as summer grass. Feels like perfect ending, though now is just beginning. At some moment, arbitrary as rain, I will kiss the blue nylon of her Hollywood shades and slide away. Now. I raise my head, pull my feet from tangled flannel sheets. Now

another pewter-toned rush hour
                                          along that strip of Venables
traffic slowing to a morning trickle stops me full
just outside Busy Kitchen Grill (breakfast $3.50)
I scan a sleeping cat
              stretched large on the sidewalk
                                    paws to the road
I grip the driver's wheel   wait

            wait—
                        not a cat

for battered women good news today
        the car radio announces
                    as my eyes begin to see

battered   the word grabs me hard
                                                from behind
whoever sees a battered woman
        she doesn't much appear in the public eye

as my eyes . . .
            a racoon instead
                                    not sleeping
strip of grass beneath its head
                in the protective angle of cement
a dark round red
            bubble of blood in its mouth
            crabapple tucked into white frill of teeth

I look away   then make myself look back:

how this animal has arranged itself against the wall
so not to draw the eye
to look ordinary
            like a cat sleeping
      black band eyes   ticked fur   composed   still

      on my way to work
      the trucks   the cars
      car radio   bubble of blood

At 62 he had his first heart attack. I wasn't there.
My sister saw his face fade grey. Sat with him in the Chrysler on the way to
the hospital in Lachine. Twenty minutes. My mother driving.

For two weeks the stubble salted on his jaw.
His cheeks concaved. Stopped smoking. Stopped working. To hold back
death.

For years before his heart attack he sells sanitation supplies. Works overtime,
evenings, weekends. Industrial floor polisher demonstrations, in his grey suit
pants, white shirt sleeves rolled to the elbows. Mouth pursed as he swings
the large silver machine first right then left in circles over the lobby floor,
a handful of building maintenance men waiting to judge the high-shine
results. Vinyl tiles giving back his reflection. Gets home some nights after
8. Eats supper with me and my sister for hungry company. S'more Daddy?
He piles his fork with mashed turnip. I lean in, open wide. My mother at
the sink. The four of us in the kitchen under the overhead fluorescent panel.
Window over the sink letting in a square of black shiny night.

He worked for Avmor. I can still dry my hands under their hand-dryers on
the BC ferries. He praised his products, even at our kitchen table. Every sale
an applause. Went in Saturday mornings in his dark fedora. Black slip-on
rubbers like thin skins over his leather shoes in winter, the kind that got
lost in thick cold puddles on Dorchester Street. You'd come across them
lost at the curb, drowning in the slush.

Drove the 2 & 20 to his work in the middle of the business district. Office
in a crumbling Old Montreal building. The way he romanticized his places.
Made them sound biblical. Black and soft brown sepia.

Bought a new Dodge every other year. Later Chryslers. Predictable as June.

19

I drive my 15 year old Japanese import down the ramp to the underground parking. Break. Slide my personal access card into the grim black mouth of the card reader in the cement wall. I've edged extra close so I can insert my card all the way in. Its right eye blinks green. The steel garage door clanks up slowly, a medieval portcullis. Ease down the ramp. Into underground dark. Swing hard right into #19, snug beside the cement pillar.

Managers can be early but never late. Never late and don't leave early. I drag home files. Forget breaks. Attend lunchtime meetings, spooning my yogurt at 2:05 in the afternoon.   Hours and hours and minutes and seconds. Starting with Monday. Documents crowding my briefcase. My briefcase an albatross.

My father didn't carry a briefcase.

He walked with his head down. Fast. Hands in his pants pockets.

       while car doors slam & slam against this morning
I sound hardheels
     sharp
         against the concrete floor

sparrows nest inside this underground parkade
     shadow-wing my morning eyes
          seduce my morning purpose   my resolve

         cavebirds   right through
            the steel grid doors

As I grew older he embarrassed me more. My father trying to fit in. Obvious. Picking up conversations with strangers in elevators, trapping them with his banter. Did you hear the one about the Irish jockey? I watched his talker ways in the world of sidewalks, lobbies, parking lots. His job in the business district at the bottom of Beaver Hall Hill, how he said Beaver Hall Hill in rounded capital letters. His stylish suits. His new cars. His jokes.

How he did. How he didn't. Fit in. Outside the house. And inside.

How his messages did. Fit into me.

My mother in the centre of the house.

waking at night
to dark edge of duvet
beginning (again) to calculate
                amount of my
(approaching) pension:
2% x number of years worked x average
best 5 years' salary = beat of rain
                        at bedroom window
with 15% penalty for collecting early + roll in my CPP – OAS
until I'm 65 (my forehead straining) = rain cascading
                        from the eaves outside
tax and benefits
        are they deducted?
start again: 2% x each year worked – one year on leave =
rain   a tattoo
            is dental still included?
full awake and urgent
start again:
            waking at night
            edge of dark duvet

At the breakfast table his mash of soft boiled egg.
His face shiny with his lotion.

The smell.

Shaving nick   red   on his chin

Applies the membrane of his soft boiled egg to staunch the bleeding.

Sales on his mind   traffic   commissions

                    the rush of his leaving
                        the "where's my goddamn . . . ?"

    It's raining.
    His shoulders hunch against the rain as he walks to his car.

                    My mother his only door back.

They say that workers in the 19th century smashed the clocks over the factory doors.

They say the Navajo language has no word for time.

That the Japanese have a word for death by overwork: *karoshi*. Finding them sprawled over their desks in corporate devotion. In North America we have no word, only heart failure. A failure of the heart.

The Gutenberg presses printed calendars before they printed bibles.

They say the Bushmen of the Kalahari spend only 10% of their waking hours sustaining themselves.

I say I spend 60% waking hours in an office or a meeting room painted grey or some off-shade of white with tired air crusting yellow round the edges and dark patterned wall-to-walls with clocks on walls clicking the time with headaches spiking round my eyes and 30 other eyes behind 15 pairs of glasses and coffee cups, Nalgene water bottles and ballpoint pens and pilots in the palm, blackberries, many stories up.

They say the windows never open. This high up someone might jump.

I park my car in #19. Check the time. Check the load on my passenger seat. My sprawling briefcase. Cracking black leather so cheap it's almost cardboard, but tough. Front compartment bulges open, can't snap shut. Never meant to be a suitcase, a purse substitute. Heavy, it could be a fitness program. And a purple cotton lunch bag; inside the bag a sliced turkey sandwich same as yesterday, and a yogurt.

I walk the smooth concrete to the two elevator doors side by side. Which door will open first? A trivial game involving positioning. Small crate of an elevator, no ceiling. High up, overhead, all the elevator wires and metal pads remain exposed as if the workmen are on a long-gone coffee break. It's always like that. I press the close-door button. If I don't, the doors stay open too long. A time thing. Now that I'm at work. Doors need closing. Fast.

Walk past reception. Three dark-haired women stand or sit at phones behind the long mahogany curve of the reception desk.

Sandra. Renée. Barbara.

Behind them, north-facing windows. Mountains and tall buildings light their days.

"Morning." "Morning." "Morning."

Divas of reception. I nod to each.

Long grey corridor. Carpet charcoal with mauve flecks. Plum-coloured woodwork trim. These colours whisper: get down to business. They whisper it all day long.

Walls of glass for each office. We watch each other float or swim or sink. Mine is the 6th glass office, north side, the more important mountain view.

My office door always open. Trapping soft sounds of human voices in the corridors. Just inside my dark blue door, a small round table, four chairs for meetings. Expectant like a small party might erupt any time.

Two bookshelves with binders black and blue, all same-sized and labelled, hold each other up. A grey, standard-issue office phone sits on a small side desk. Wait till you hear it ring. A cartoon sound: gooley gooley gooley — gooley gooley gooley.

And a computer, with a screen count of 43 unread e-mails this morning. How does that happen? Do they work all night?

I nudge my briefcase behind the little telephone table near the window, out of sight. Open the bottom drawer of my desk. Reach past the rice cakes, the Anacin, the lip ointment, cough lozenges. Fiddle the opening of the box of black tea, Ridgeway's organic.

when I return from the kitchen following my mug of milky tea, someone is sitting at my desk, back to me, hunched small in dark blue serge.

it's him.

I slip into my office, sit sidesaddle at my table, lean forward and ease the door shut.

I stare at the black hair on the back of his head.

it's got to be him.

he's gazing out my window into the maroon-coloured leaves of the two-storey maple tree.

foliage like burgundy satin, dense as a jungle.

he whirls around like this is film noir.

his face white   eyes black.

he twists his mouth into a pout. bites inside his mouth, the smooth hollows of his cheeks, his mouth pulling down into a deeper twist as he bites harder. tearing off bits from inside his face and chewing. one side, and then the other. small ruminating movements of his lips. delicately eating away at himself.

Don't you worry about cancer of the mouth? Biting like that. My mother always warned me, I tell him. I tongue inside my cheeks, poke the pocked and bitten flesh.

why should i? he asks me. died of tuberculosis. remember? in an asylum. young.

Then why do you? When you have nothing left to worry about?

worry is a habit i have never abandoned. especially in the night. instilled by my father, with whom i lived all my life, until the sanatorium. though if it hadn't been my father, i would have found another source. i worry at myself, you might say, incessantly. would i know myself if i did not cannibalize myself? i enjoy the rhythm of it. soothing. i enjoy the sensation of my teeth inside something. biting into is most satisfying. teeth in charge. keeps me from screaming.

Joyce from Rehab Services and Lillian in Human Resources rap at my window-wall. Point to their watches.

Late? For what? I must have forgotten.

They cradle folders, stacks of papers. They gesture down the corridor toward the boardroom.
I nod up and down in the same exaggerated way they have been pointing, miming through the window-wall. In continuous motion, they arrow away. Joyce arcs back, tilts her quizzical head. A sheet of paper floats off the top of her pile, waves, flutters past the glass out of sight.

See what I mean? I turn to Kafka. At the same time rummaging for my daytimer.

i know very well what you mean. worked for years in offices.   built my reputation on it.

I don't say my colleagues are not gracious. (I want him to know.) They also smile and laugh, despite. They are my friends. One day they will enter
                    the kingdom of heaven or some kind of pension plan.
They want to help people. They endure these corridors, suffering in ways beyond their admission.
I don't say my work is not worthwhile: people need shelter. Especially people who can't find their own.

The work is that necessary.

That tedious.

At the age of 7 I played House with my sister in our bedroom. Shoving furniture around to shape walls and doors. Names at make-believe doors written on the backsides of night tables in black crayon: The Browns. The Greys. The Blacks.

Houses formed by night tables in a room which was a street.

How are you today Mrs. Brown?

Fine thank-you and you Mrs. Grey?

But what of Mr. Brown? Mr. Grey? This question should be asked.

No Mr. Brown, no Mr. Grey, not in this game. This is daytime, they'd be at the office.

We played House, School, Store, Queen of the Fairies. We did not play Office.

No one we knew played Office. Who would play Office?

I am always on trial I complain to him.

Some days no matter how many meetings I attend
I find it's not enough.   No matter how many phone calls
I take I find the phone keeps ringing. No matter how much I read, no matter
how much I talk, no matter how much I plan, how much I write, how many
clothes I wear, miles I drive, lunches I miss, I find it's not enough.

Always my belly weeping. My belly full of days.

he looks into his hands
        folded like two shells in his lap.

                        of course you are on trial.
                        it's how it is.   this kind of place:
                        who is not on trial?

Kafka returns to the point: now that i am in your office, what do you want from me?

Help me write myself out of these corridors.

resign.   surely others do.

They pay me too well. I've been here two decades. What else do I know? What other work can I do? I'm waiting for my pension.   I have a mortgage. I eat in restaurants.   I buy tiger lilies for my spice. My pension is too small.

in this millennium you have a choice.

I have a struggle, not so much a choice, though your arrival, this beginning, is encouraging. Your name lends credibility to this project.   To write me out of here.

i will be your ghost writer. your conditions of bureaucracy intrigue me. the apparati of this century are momentous. i have modernized my writing style, trivial, but literature has its fashions. still my method is to dream. with remarkable ease in my current state, and though composing can be tedious i have started. i will immerse myself in your milieu.   i will scribe you to your end, which may or may not suit you.   but preference is overrated, in these times.

he slips a yellow folder from my desk, then disappears from the bottom up, like the Cheshire cat without the smile, his mouth moving, a talking head, asking if i have located the beginning, but not waiting for my answer.

When my mother died my father said:
Your mother had no money of her own.
Not true. This much I know.   She told me.
She kept a small account of savings
                    bought cheaper teas and socks on sale.
In case.

She said don't tell your father.

He said: How could she, your mother never worked.

Not true.   She worked:
                    darned his socks
                    reupholstered his chair
                    trimmed the hedge
                    dusted the dressers
                    simmered pot roasts
                    found the scissors
                    the needle and the thread
                    stitched
                    all the disparate pieces back;
she worked to make him whole
                    and whole again
            at the end
                of every day.

At 22 I visited my father's office. I wanted to see his places. 1969—I wore a brown felt hat. With a brim and a rounded dome. He said to me: Why are you wearing that hat? A hippie hat.

I had walked all the way from Sherbrooke Street down Beaver Hall Hill to Old Montreal. Wearing my first born on my back and a miniskirt and a brown felt hat. The office grey with grey lino, scuffed, and old oak desks and kitchen chairs, and high ceilings that bloomed with fluorescent panel hum. The air was two centuries old. It smelled of mould and overflowing ashtrays, old floor wax and men. Salesmen in white and blue dress shirts, sleeves rolled, hands in pockets, nodding when they said, Your daughter? Shaking my hand. Uh huh, looking at me and at him. Yup, Tom's daughter. Ties loose round their necks. Phone ringing somewhere in a back office.

Some days
     time runs you down like a runaway car
Some days
     it lies still as mirrored windows
flat as silver coins

Some days both

Monday—
     check your e-mail
     check your watch
     watch your cheque
     in a meeting watch the clock
     watch a wall a mouth moving
     watch pairs of eyes
          flat as coins

          check the muscles of your mouth
          the tendons in your neck

Monday afternoon
glimpse me striding
                    past
                        the ED's office door
see how fasssst
in my black suit   earrings silver flashing
        I flash   my lips   my hard-heeled shoes
eyeballs   forward   briefcase swinging
                                headlong out the door

knowing the speed of highway traffic
                        racing   crackling   skidding
focused as teeth
                    a metronome mid-sentence   mid-step
words spin in half sentences   change policy on access   hire part-time
staff   speak   pant   sign   contracts memos letters reports
                                                faster   faster
            money racing   a river underground
            plan propose promote conclude
            new services   new homes   year round
                                            year end
bury dollars count cents hedge bets build apartments houses shelters

imperative: move people   more people into better places   better faster
before they get hooked or hurt or sent back to hospitals   before the money
disappears   again   year end   into someone else's budget
                                watch how fassst in my black suit

nothing brief about this black case   though outside is nothing much
inside is all I ever need in case:

I tube of lip balm 7 pens 4 pencils right front pouch I pack of
Trident cherry gum   pack of Kleenex   roll of Tums   Anacin   cell
phone in mid compartment but not the zippered mid compartment
3 thin packs of Sweet 'NLow   I hot pink safety-whistle   daytimer in the zippered middle 2 steno pads heavy metal key-chain-
weapon ('The Cat') with 2 sharp ears and large-holed eyes for
index and my middle fingers when the parkade mugger says don't
move calculator snuggled beside cell phone   wallet an open mouth
cheque book passport turkey sandwich apple can of diet Pepsi
5 folders colour-coded   yellow for finance red for agency blue for
correspondence   green for work-to-bring-home   work-to-bring-
in work-to-solve work-to-plan   orange for work-to-carry-around
sometimes a navy sweater sometimes Emily Dickinson

case for:

old friend   I can toss it on the back seat of the car   it doesn't
whimper   no alligators skinned in its construction   no pigs no
sheep no kids no albatross no eels were killed or dyed   my honey-
spice bought it for me when I started this big job so I'd fit in it lives
at the end of my arm   its handle in my leather glove or sweating
palm according to the season   commodious as an old oak desk

case against:

a cow was killed in its construction but so old so tough hide heavy
now scuffed and beaten   hide-away-behind-the-desk hide broken
hide make or break case lower case stocky as a steer zipper refuses
front pouch refuses closure   pens leak out and pencils unpadded
handles bite my palms heavy as a heifer droops my shoulders
pulls my neck bangs my knee   never lets me out of its sight   like
wall street cuffs   my albatross everything inside somewhere

In a dream my father asks: why are you wearing my brown fedora?

Are you sure this hat belongs to you? I ask him

My mother enters. She says: She needs a hat, Tom. Now that she is working.

I want to explain to my mother that we don't wear hats to work, but she would feel corrected.

I wear so many hats, I say to my father. How can you be sure this one is yours? It could be my own from years ago, that hippie hat, remember? It could be K's. He wears a fedora.

Who is K? my parents lower their brows at me.

Before I can explain, my father's blue eyes lighten. He says: you can wear my brown fedora.

Tuesday morning meeting. Walls oyster grey. Greyday glare from north-facing windows obscures pale glassy watercolours hanging on opposite wall. Bright panels of chromium cubes light the ceiling. Department Head at head of mahogany table presenting this week's corporate directions. Words jingle from her mouth.

14 of us watch her. Including a man in a worsted blue suit with narrow lapels. His head is down. The rest of us watch those words come whole, from her red and wholesome mouth. Nodding our heads. Eyes forward. Mouths curving down. Papers spreading white and cornered. Some, nodding, writing down her words. To hear them jingle some day from their own downturned mouths: performance expectations budget responsibilities corporate vision grievance management standards of excellence employee files mission statement fiscal accountability time management restructuring (for efficiencies) strategic planning

In my mind I count backward, buying time (tomorrow being 191), playing with my too-tight watch-band. 8:48:23 AM

Then, 8:49:17, picking up my pen,

write: Tuesday morning meeting. Walls oyster grey.
        Greyday glare from northfacing windows
        obscures pale glassy watercolours on opposite
        wall. Bright panels of chromium cubes
        light the ceiling. Department Head at head
        of mahogany table presenting this week's
        corporate directions. Words jingle from her
        mouth. . . .

I tell no one about Kafka. Not my spice who smiles at me blondly from the side of a granite mountain. Not my two sons or my grandson, each watching me from behind their own framed squares of protective glass. Not my colleagues who pop in to share traffic information, accounts of rain, last night's *Survivor*.

I am already partial enough.

How my father used to say: The customer is always right. Here, customers (though we prefer the term 'client') ask for locks on their care home bedroom doors, want to make decisions about taking medication, want to have a say. Here, not everyone agrees that the client is always right. They cite legal concerns, call client requests naive, inconvenient, subversive. I believe the customer is right. Most of the time.

They can't know about Kafka. He would not fit in. Dead for decades.

Still.

My watch ticks the days away and my paycheque passes through my fingers fast as beads spill off a string. Days spent, paycheques spent, and me. Which is the point of this equation.

I focus on the money-made part of the equation: wait for payday, go to the bank, study the balance, count the numbers.

I count the dollars to keep me safe. In case. In case the roof leaks or the car stalls or thunder strikes or the bottom falls out.

I count the numbers to keep me rewarded: take my girlfriend to the Café de Paris, drive to the Rockies, see *La Traviata* from the middle seats.

I count to stay included, keep the phone ringing, the e-mails coming in.

In the Classic Comic, Silas Marner sits on his cabin floor counting gold. Like it's evil. Call it greed. Call it business sense. Call it profit motive. Call it fear.

My father lived through the Depression; he always turned out lights I had left on. A quirk, just another habit.

Part Two
SPIRAL DOWN

In 16th century Italy the authorities incarcerate a certain man. In Venice. After twenty years the authorities cannot remember why the man is confined. The magistrate tells him he can leave. The guards leave the door to his cell open. The man sees the door is open but the man does not leave. His cousin comes to get him. But the man shakes his head, remains inside his cell seated on his wooden bench. He tells his cousin he will not leave. He cannot leave. The door stays open. He will not cross the threshold into the courtyard beyond.

Every other Thursday morning Doris flipped
an envelope into my inbox—standard white—
here it is! she said, said:
this is what it's all about!
Every other Thursday Doris smiled broad like paycheque Santa.
Hip-hip-hooray cheque, this-is-the-day cheque, what-d'ya-say cheque.
Cocked her head. Flourished the Thursday envelope. White paper flag.
Said: here's what makes it all worthwhile.   And laughed.

                It's not a paycheque anymore. It's a pay-
                stub which only rhymes with grub or nub or sub or tub or
                        rub or pub, a simple
                paper trail
                a reckoning for April's income tax.   And Doris doesn't
                        work here anymore.

Turns out time does not only careen or lie still. Like something frozen left too long in a self-defrosting fridge, it desiccates. One breath at a time. Gone. Gone again. Flakes and disappears. At the end of the day I look back at nothing. No A to B. No silvered peace. Only deflation.

Afraid one day I'll let my mouth say something wrong. Let go for a second. Silk scarf undone Slipping from the throat. My ragged self revealed. Everything ruined.
Ashamed to feel this afraid.
Except for paycheque loss,
what's to fear?
Ashamed to notice how afraid I sometimes feel.

I say they pay me too much, too much to leave: I am now too
accustomed to the state of acquisition. The state of ease.
I like gold frames. I do. And silver. Italianate perhaps. Bordering, let's say,
a sacred grouping chosen for their particular and superior credentials of
service and loyalty to much higher causes.
Chosen also for good bones and Arcadian cheeks.

I too am framed in gold.
Though I like it less and less, complaining and fearful, still I have
consumer preferences.

The other side of the coin.
(We all have an underside.)

This is universal (if such a thing as universal still remains).

The details are a matter of taste.
Some prefer the Bauhaus.

When the countdown zeroed out and I still parked my car in stall 19, it became clear I would not leave this place by counting off the days, as though they formed a simple row of beads. Time shifted, revealing itself to be no longer a rosary, a meaningful chain. No longer a rigid length of time, a straight-edged ruler or a knife. No longer 206 or 205.

Somehow, dollars began to count more than days. For one thing, the Pension Corporation (formerly the Superannuation Commission), after months of phone calls from me requesting precision (as in exactly how much per month) sent a letter (their preferred way of doing business) to reveal an amount much less than I had calculated (using 2% per year of contribution). Because I propose to retire early. There is a penalty. The final risk. One day, as the count reached zero, the fear swelled fat as a delirium. Again.

When the counting ended, the days surfaced all the same again, Monday was as Tuesday and Wednesday was as Thursday, without meaning except the dreary rhythm of their recited names, even Saturday and Sunday, being part of the cycle, were the same. None was called 206 or 205 or 191. Round and round the Mondays bobbed without progression. The ancient mariner in an ocean of corridors. Briefcase around my neck. No land, no more, in sight.

I have been chewing again on the soft insides of my mouth. Sometimes I draw blood. When I finish with my mouth, I gnaw my wrists, my ankles. I demolish calloused fingers, thumbs, the skin around my nails.

I'll be sitting in a meeting watching someone's mouth open and close around words like "accountability" and "outcome measures." My right thumb at rest against my chin, slips closer to my mouth. Trapping the skin on my thumb pad between my front teeth, I keep my eyes on the speaker. A matter of precision, I close my teeth against the minuscule wedge of thumb skin and tear it off. Looking thoughtful, pretending not to be doing this childish thing. Strategy and necessity from my early years.

if it relieves anxiety it is worthwhile, says Kafka, sitting at my desk again one Saturday when I drop in to finalize my Annual Report.

These days, I tell him, we're advised to run or join an aerobics class. Stress management techniques are encouraged everywhere. Along with plenty of bottled water.
I drop my briefcase at his feet.

i set my watch one hour and a half ahead, which helps me be prepared; we all practice our own form of release, he responds.   in practice for the end.

Which end do you mean? I am more adrift than ever, no end in sight, now even without my linear longing.

story's end, which this is about. all parts of writing story are mysterious, he tells me, but the end is by far the most strenuous. it must be crafted flawlessly. the writer must be committed. thereafter, turning back is hazardous. i continue to dream and write; i hope you do too. my materialization is sporadic, but soon there will be an ending. i've left you the beginning . . .

My phone rings, gooley, gooley, gooley, is always ringing. Gooley gooley.

Excuse me, I say to him, and turn to pick up the phone.

Can I call you back? I ask the receiver.

Immediately, this is Finance. Yes, on Saturday.

When I turn around, an air patch shimmers and I see his fingers still curled on the table top, disappearing one by one.

Of course.

My mind filling with the gnash and whirr of teeth.

The phone again.
Finance again.

As I replace the receiver, I notice a yellow folder on my table. He's left me something at last, which, despite my Annual Report, I read immediately:

At the first stoplight, Frances dug into her briefcase for Anacin and downed two tablets before the light changed. At the second, she cleared her throat and started her scales. Her voice teacher, Madame Brod, advised her that regular practice was necessary for her progress, especially with lieder music, of which Frances was now so fond. As the traffic slowed for a bus leaving the curb, she wondered what other commuters thought of her mouthings. She prayed none of her management team colleagues would pull up beside her. She hoped her parents would find an apartment of their own, soon.

She hadn't shared her new obsession with the team. Why should she? They wouldn't understand. Sure, they acknowledged that interests outside the office were healthy; the Stress Reduction Consultant advised managers to take up hobbies to counter the demands of the workplace. But Frances knew that hiking and book clubs were one kind of hobby, healthy and neutral, lieder music and voice lessons were quite another. There was nothing neutral about lieder for Frances; she depended on it.

But Germanic tunes had gained an unfortunate reputation recently among her colleagues. Strange unpredictable musical interludes, often lieder tunes, had plagued their office building for more than a month. It all started in early January. Paul, in Policy and Research, suspected that the music was piped in through the heating system and Jim told everyone that they were in a collective trance. No one was able to solve the mystery; the music interrupted now as if it were a normal part of the work day.

As she steered around the corner of Larch and 12th, a strange thought popped into Frances' head: was the mystery music connected somehow with her own interest in lieder? The mid-week commute was coagulating. She honked her horn at a Jag. It's because I 've started singing. She knew it was crazy. I'll lose my mind next; I've got to get out of this job. But then Gregor came to mind, and her parents, who were staying with them until they found something affordable. She thought of the people who benefitted from the work she did and of the homeless in the news this morning. They depended on her. She drove the rest of the way grinding her teeth.

As she drove into the underground parkade, organ music filled her ears. The music was loudest in the building parkade. Some staff had started to take the bus and others now parked in an nearby parking lot on Heather St. The pounding of organ keys became more determined, menacing as the sound track for Jaws.

Inside the elevator, the music muted, another tune, more like a Muzak version of a funeral march. Though it didn't bother Frances as much as it bothered others, she was relieved when she stepped off the elevator onto her own floor and the hollow rhythms halted altogether.

The other managers' office doors were closed, but she knew they were in their offices working. She glimpsed their dark suits through the staggered panels of sand-blasted glass. 7:10 and they're here already, annoyed with herself for being the last in and the others for being there at all. She had 14 voice messages waiting and 54 e-mail messages. Her inbox spilled over into her outbox. She placed her briefcase behind her desk and opened the blue folder to the agenda for this morning's meeting. A rising solo horn, forlorn and haunting, pierced her office's quiet.

Frances walked into her morning meeting as the music stopped again. It had a way of starting and stopping mid-note. When the hell will it stop, muttered Paul Greenwood, Public Relations Manager, ignoring the fact that it had. He was always the first at this weekly meeting. He always sat in the same seat, facing the clock. Steam circled his bald head as he blew into his green and white paper cup. Marg, the secretary for the meeting, smiled at him and lifted her own green and white cup to her glossy red lips. Despite his scowl, he winked back.

The rest of the management team drifted into leather chairs around the long mahogany table. Outside, eight stories up, a slow drizzle shrouded the floor-to-ceiling windows. They were sitting in the clouds. The world disappeared.

Frances brought the meeting to order at 8:15. In the initial check-in round, Jim Masters and Ron Beacon, both Financial Managers, reported losing a number of confidential documents. Three highly confidential documents disappeared on Thursday, said Ron. Stolen right off my desk. I've started locking my door.

Sure you didn't misplace them? asked Frances.

Same thing happened to me, said Jim. On Friday. Sheila can't find them and I need them for the audit.

The managers looked around the table, jutting their chins, swivelling their heads to follow each speaker as they debated the question of office security, which included the vexing fact that no one had solved the issue of the underground music. They cleared their throats and removed their jackets, now all talking at once. As meeting chair, Frances raised her voice, hoping to redirect them back to the agenda. Finally she slapped the table with her right hand. Let's break for fifteen. We'll hear from Planning when we get back. She kept her left hand coiled in her lap.

Her mother had dinner waiting in the oven for Frances when she arrived home that evening. Always so late, marvelled her mother, and she lowered a plate of ham and scalloped potatoes, frilled around the edges, to the dining-room table. Since they'd moved to Vancouver to escape Ontario winters, her parents had taken over Frances' domestic life. It made her feel like a kid.

She hung her coat in the hall closet and sat down. It was 8:15.

Gregor called! her mother shouted from the kitchen. So sweet, that boy; he staying two weeks longer than he thought though.

Frances knew this from their last call. Maybe she'd check out weekend flights to New Mexico if she could get away.

How was apartment hunting today? Frances shouted from the dining room.

Your singing keeps up, dear, we'll be forced to take anything; Dad's in bed with a sick headache. You know how he hates music, she reminded Frances. She entered the dining room with a heaping dish of rocky road ice cream. No apartments so far, she said.

That's too much, said Frances.

It's your favourite, dear.

It's Dad's favourite.

Frances ate her ice cream, then called Gregor. His answering machine told her he was out. Oh Gregor, her mouth on the receiver, and then she sang, "oft denk' ich, sie sind nur ausgegangen! Bald werden sie wieder nach Hause gelangen!" her voice filled with sober lieder feeling as it drew out each flattened syllable. Then she sang it again in English, "I often think they have only gone out: soon they will come home again." It was their private joke. "Goodnight Gregor," she said. She brushed her teeth and went to bed early. She felt a headache creeping around her hairline.

The next day, Frances received a stern e-mail advising all staff that security measures would be upgraded. This included standard procedures such as hiring a renowned firm of security consultants and increasing the number of security guards patrolling the building. Frances patted the ID card hanging around her neck. New measures also included, she read, further restricting access to various parts of the building. The last paragraph described a new plan to construct a moat around the perimeter of the building. A moat? She wanted to laugh. They can't be serious. An international engineering company, responsible for industrial security moat construction in Japan, Hong Kong and Switzerland, had been identified to provide a proposal for the moat project. She didn't laugh.

Before she left the office that evening, Frances learned that the moat would be stocked with alligators, like the prototype in Hong Kong. She made no complaint, of course, but she couldn't stop thinking about the alligators. From the time her mother had taken her to see Peter Pan, Frances had harboured a brooding fear of crocodiles.

Crocodiles and clocks, her mother said that evening when they discussed the moat, which had been featured on the local evening news. Although, my dear, you've adjusted nicely to clocks, right? Her mother tilted her head toward Frances. Wrong, Frances thought, I still hate clocks. Ticking, timing, out to get her.

Her mother put down her knitting and rubbed her hands, one over the other, as though washing them. She straightened up and rolled her shoulders back. Frances could hear them crack and crunch. She picked up her knitting again, the needles clicking and rocking, rocking and clicking. Alligators and crocodiles are so similar, she said, like peas in a pod. Can't tell the difference myself. And what about caymans? Just smaller, right? She smiled a caymanish smile.

I want you to use this opportunity, dear, to overcome your crocodilophobia, her mother advised. Make us even prouder. She placed her knitting in her dainty lap and wiped *away a tear. She was knitting something small and yellow. Frances didn't want to know what it was.*

Her father's shaggy eyebrows appeared over the top of his newspaper, billowed broad as a sail in his hammy hands. He nodded, just once, but emphatically. She knew Gregor would be kind, but he might side with her parents. She supposed it was for her own good. She needed to come to terms, as they said, with her demons.

That night as she unclasped the gold hoops, first one and then the other earlobe fell off, hoops still attached. In the mirror, she rearranged her streaked hair to cover her ears. If she didn't move her head too quickly, her new forward hairstyle stayed in place. She'd use hair spray in the morning. She removed the hoops from the earlobes and placed them in their separate jewellery box compartments.

She had now a growing collection of body bits, all hers. She puzzled about the lack of blood or pain. On a scrap of paper she made a note to herself to call her doctor in the morning. Despite the demands on her time, these incidents were beginning to alarm her. One day someone would notice that parts of her were missing. Just as well that Gregor was away until the end of the following month.

✵ ✵ ✵

When I finally answer the phone, my tongue sticks to my teeth, my fingertips burn cold. Who is Frances Keegan?

In the middle of my need to end, I find only this piece of middle story, without beginning and without end, which is no answer at all.

They laid off the man in the office next to mine. The man who always wore a striped tie. Before they laid him off, they ignored him. They did not invite him to meetings. He received no e-mails. He joined no corridor huddles. He bought take-out from the Korean Café two doors away, ate lunches at his desk, door closed, the muted sounds of easy listening radio oozing out. On some afternoons, I heard him shouting into the phone. Through his closed door, I could hear him swearing.

You're lucky, we said to him.
Be able to do anything you want.
Which was true. Almost anything
Anything except work at his job and collect his paycheque.
Which we did not say to him.

We know something else (which we do not even say to each other):
That we are lucky. Those chosen to work. Even though.
To whatever degree, we are the ones in the boardroom. In the offices, with Visas in our wallets. And golden frames on living room walls. Or Bauhaus sofas.
To whatever degree, we fit. Enough.
He does not. Anymore.

Others do not either. Ever. I see them on the street. Leaning on shopping carts filled with plastic bags and dark coats and old pants. I watch them huddle in doorways, circle the front doors of downtown shelters. No rooms of their own.

What we learned in Grade One, what the memos still say: some fit, some do not.
Work is like religion; you are expected to believe, to belong. As a person wanting to fit in, I am not righteous. Not even faithful. Do not wholly believe the social codes, the work ethics. I harbour false pretenses. I dread discovery.

                    I hurry the block with my banging black briefcase
to Starbucks for latté   decaf low-fat
                    or to London Drugs for Cozaar on the Extended Plan
                    past a row of stores
          where 2 or 3   on pavement with crossed legs
at intervals with signs that read: I need
                    money for food   I am homeless
                            the woman strokes a red-bandanna'd dog
I drop her a loonie   smile   I mean it   step over the bandanna'd dog

when I was young a boy sold yellow pencils
from his wheelchair
                    on St. Catherine Street in Montreal
lived in a mansion my mother said, wary of lies,
said she'd seen him walk
                    to his chauffeured limo
5 PM one winter day.

Will I survive another 206 or 103 or 64 days that solid block of rented time get out of bed   put on my navy suit my pearls my rings thread through morning traffic choked with SUV's and small import cars   read agency annual reports plan budgets for new staffing write program changes again again write memos to the boss monitor finances enforce another policy attend 5 meetings 6 meetings every day   5 days a week   make lists   make like I like it again again

Will I make it to the end?

How will the ending read?

K: ending is not yet on the page.

Don't assume I am ungrateful. As partial employment-heretic, I'm grateful to be allowed inside the sanctums of these buildings, receive bi-monthly cheques. Remain undiscovered. Although everyday the grey on these walls causes me to catch my breath. Grey is not a colour that belongs to me. And everyday cheerleader colleagues pom-pom the halls and set my icy teeth to mute. And everyday these 8-foot windows cause me to think of trees. And clouds. And flight. My unfitness tucked tight under my arms, I fit nowhere. Do not believe enough in the corporate new clothes. Or in the colour grey. I question more than I believe. My corporate faith is insufficient.

In the more inquisitive 16th century, after twenty years of incarceration, they would have located my unbelief. The exact organ of its origin. My liver perhaps. Or my spleen. They would have burned my paycheque at the stake, eaten my rebellious roasted heart. Long before doors opened.

He gets off the elevator with me and shoulder to shoulder we hurry to my office. His fedora brim drips, his tight blue suit darkened with rain.

You're not well enough to go out in this weather, I say to him.

He pulls a cotton handkerchief from his pant pocket and coughs into it. Folds it in quarters. Pockets it.

How about a cup of tea, coffee? I ask him. Then I pull out my bottle of Anacin and gulp them from my cupped hand. I force them down by swallowing twice, hard. I replace the cap and shove the plastic bottle back in the drawer. I need another bottle, I mutter, almost to him, to me.

you take too many pills, he admonishes me.

Headaches, I say. Gets me through the afternoon. And a cup of tea. I'll get one for you too.

soon you'll have ulcers too.

I have blood pressure too. I take a morning pill for that.

pills, pills, pills. have you nothing more organic, less invasive?

Massages. Physiotherapy. I use those treatments already. But nothing works like pills. I had a wry neck last year and took muscle relaxants but got a rash. I had to stop. The wry neck was very painful. And of course, I rarely sleep. But I don't take sleeping pills. Yet.

i know about pain. and about not sleeping. and about stomach problems. and about treatments. you have to be vigilant.

And get out of this job, I say.

before you end up like me.

crab-scuttle dry leaves a jazz riff
            keyed low on the sidewalk   wind spins
      as the coffee shop door blows me
                        into the Bergman shot   clouds scudding
            remember   if nothing else   this wind   wild today
      which disassembles   without which
                  not even me   now my scoured eyes
            sunlight too like a palomino
gallops in my hair   tugs across cool   this way   that
                        a rearrange of morning brushwork
         which cools the backs of my hands
                  as I try to catch lapels
                        as jacket flaps wide

         which opens my head
                  my throat

                  without which I remain intact only
                  without which I walk alone   without
dry brown scuttle spin and whoop this bright
                              blue whipped
                              skull ripped
                                             wide
                        this diamond day

first there was a mink stole in a colour called champagne
sleek as a Hollywood starlet
but her unmarried sisters both layawayed their mink stoles too

her idea with the mink stole
was to cut herself
                   out of the family crowd
make her better than her two sisters who
for some reason thought they were better
                                    than her

so then there was the mink jacket   brown with full collar   cuffs
                    three-quarter length
but the two sisters both purchased jackets too
brown collars   deep cuffs

it made outdoing them more necessary than ever

my modest mother knew what must be done—
                        a Florida condo
her sisters had their fiscal limits
                        2 bedrooms   pool   east coast
to heck with the heat   she'd bring the stole

all in how you define success: what you want, what your parents wanted, what you get used to:
the way I count my bank account in multiples of 1000
the way I say the title of my job
how we buy a new Scandinavian cherry wood dining-room table with blue upholstered chairs drink green apple martinis shaken from a silver shaker
prefer gold frames
art in the original
accumulate college degrees
spend 2 weeks in the Rockies
how my honey can always buy any book she wants

how my mother smiled mink in her champagne stole how my father bought a new Dodge every other year a retirement condo in Fort Lauderdale stashed dollars in the mining stocks wore flashy grey silk suits

Questions crowd: did he love us?
       If he loved us, how'd he know?
How would we know?
       My mother, my sister and me.

       My mother, my sister and me.
Did we love him? Workaholic,
where could we attach our love?
How would he know?

on this morning of agendas & coffee cups
I cannot guarantee that face across the table
    is not the face of the Virgin Mary
            in a slate blue shirt
                    hair salted falling like rain
                            past his blue shoulders

        oval   smooth-shaved as an egg
with only shadow of shadow
                    along his curving jaw
        calm as philosophy
    glasses rimless sincere
                I would let him pray for me

    our shelter, s/he is saying, is barrier-free—
    we turn away no one; each night when our beds are filled we call
                    Salvation Army or Catholic Charities
        eyes closed: they come back to us & back to us, s/he says, . . .
those men

  her face his eyes   lift   behind those lenses that do magnify
            us   our seeing   past these coffee cups
                        & words like outcome goals & waiting lists
                        this room
                        this rain

Today is Wednesday. It could have been day 52 of a second countdown, but I have no faith in counting anymore. On my way to work I see an old man on the sidewalk rolling his arms in big slow arcs around and around. His face resigned; his mouth turned down. What time did he get up this morning? It's probably Tai Chi. What time did he roll over, check the clock?

He's on the sidewalk. Morning and the city greys vast around him.

Any better that he's on the sidewalk alone going nowhere than I'm in my car alone going to work. What if it was me on the sidewalk? Rolling my arms like wheels.

What else, other than work or rolling 2 arms like intersecting wheels, fills the hours of a day? 8 or 10. I can't remember anymore.

When the time came, the guards opened the door, but the man
did not know how to leave.
His will betrayed him.

Doors open.
But no one leaves the corridors.

Doors stay open but no one crosses thresholds.

It's 6 PM. The managers remain.

Doors behind the eyes.

Cinderella complex is what they call it.   imposter, relying on fairy dust. Cinderella complex: the fear of getting caught in Walt-Disney-crayoned clothes.   how could Cinderella know how to be a princess when her childhood training was as a scullery maid? her whole princess condition dependent on a fairy godmother, a wand and a pair of slippers spun from glass. her sisters wearing champagne-coloured stoles.

how could I know how to be everything: boss, contract manager, budget planner, public speaker, decision maker, program developer, mentor, staff leader, when my girlhood scope was home? scrubbing and scrubbing to clean myself, hair, face, teeth; make myself good enough.   I befriended talking mice. I know everything about my job, but I think I only half-know everything.

my father made sinks for Crane Inc. in 1932.   he knew nothing about making sinks the first week he started to work. he wore glass shoes, but he pretended they were leather. he told it as a joke: his mistakes, how he tried to fool his bosses.

the man in the office next to me was laid off, but he did not think he was Cinderella. he yelled at his boss. he thought his boss was Cinderella, that she would change her mind before midnight.

some days who drives a pumpkin or who wears glass shoes matters more than other days. it takes a long time not to worry about working after midnight, about the silver gown dissolving into fairy dust.

My first job was making cheese sandwiches by the loaf at the Benedict Labre House. Downtown Montreal. Not so much a job, unpaid and part of our high school curriculum. Education in someone else's hardship. Liberation theology. God is everywhere, including processed cheese. We were girls, interlopers, voyeurs, without lives of our own. The men who ate the sandwiches seemed more real than us.

My first paid job was at a local swimming pool. Lifeguard. Turquoise summer suburbs, chlorinated arms, legs, hair, eyes—the smell of toxic clean. My skin so dry at the end of shift, it puckered on my bones.

Later, I taught elementary school. Boys only school. Grade Four. The boys did not speak English—they spoke Portugese, Greek, Spanish, Croatian, Italian; some were too big for their desks. At the end of every week they drew pictures of sheep in green and rolling hills.

Later, social work. Later, management. Later, administration. Black suits, silver earrings, elevators, offices with glass walls and carpets, mauve-flecked, under foot. Varying shades of real.

At 4 in the afternoon I take two more Anacin with another cup of sweet office tea. My shoulder aches. I knead it with my other hand. My neck is made of plaster. I rush back to my office, answer the phone.

As the day approached, which could have been my end, I floated in an infinity of white-space massing over my head and under my feet, curling around each fingertip. How will I live a life when I leave, when I have no work: know what time to get out of bed, where to walk, who to call, what to say to people at parties. How will I account for myself, or buy new running shoes?

Meeting drones, snakes well-past end-time. Skies
skirt dark on the wet side of office windows. The blazed
flourescents, the migraine pitch. End
of day, end of meeting well past the promised time.

Homeward at the well-past time through rain-
specked streets, through black splash and shine. Wipers
metronome the CBC. Imagining her
well-past-promised eyes: the hour, the dinner set,
the company. Remembering then to stop
for cake, two sourdough baguettes.

Home: red wine and guests through to kitchen sink.
Things ablaze: her cheeks, her mouth.
My coat flung. The cake, the two baguettes. Her crackle
touch. My promise, another, and another in the morning.

When I am home, her expectation hovers.

I hover too, between her and my yawning briefcase.

My father was Irish Catholic. My mother Irish Protestant. What they called in those days a mixed marriage. Made all the difference, that difference in religion. The Irish conflict erupting in our suburban home. Religion came to me as conflict. There were loyalties and choices, beliefs attached to each parent. Just as there are loyalties and beliefs attached to work. Another place to belong. Whether we believe in it or not.

My sister admired her First Communion gloves, white lace with cuffs, and her little white missal with its pearlized cover. Inside, pastel illuminations of saints with roses and big sad eyes. Her rosary beads like tiny glass seeds, joined by a silver cross with Christ on it. His tiny silver form spread on the silver bars. She hid them from my mother. My mother had her limits.

Just before my ninth birthday, on the first day of school, my father stood up from his soft boiled egg and announced: You girls better hurry. I'm driving you over to St. Joseph's this morning. You'll be going to the Catholic school now.

We looked at our mother wiping her kitchen counter. He could have said: I'm driving you to Russia this morning, or to Pluto, for all the sense it made.

She nodded once, like a vanquished queen, like Boadicea, pissed off, but aware of the odds. It wasn't her religion or her decision. It was his, and his behind-the-scenes Catholic mother's. And in some offstage battle they had dispersed her armies. While we slept in our beds.

Irish history. Now we are Catholics. Insiders. Outsiders.

I just wanted to be saved. I hid my need for heaven from my mother. She was Protestant; she thought saved meant more money in her secret bank account.   She might have been right.

most days I go to work in black
a habit   most of us wear black or grey or brown
to be taken seriously
Joyce prefers navy with white collars
Lillian wears charcoal and patent leather shoes
Jim and Tom and Jack
wear black   a shade of special meaning
Reneé wears brown
Sandra's days are beige
I'm in black with silver earrings
sometimes I wear a string of pearls
we dress seriously
habitually

I crossed a boundary into faith Catholics being more insistent and the whole unholy world began to tilt aunts taunted friends faded my mind minded codes choosing to believe yet years later something like doubt one drip at a time holds me back the beginning of my holding back of disbelief of being out and in at the same time still wanting something to be true wanting that full and holy feeling immersion still to give myself to higher causes higher and higher to know I'm safe eventually that wanting disappears too eventually I can be anywhere and still hold back

playing safe survival tactics bless me through years like I belong when filling up with doubt loss of that belief to buoy me through the days the faith that this work I do this time I count this place this ideal is good or good enough or any use at all

in North America when women finally entered the workplace in large numbers, as though they now stood equal, the women approached the work seriously. in the offices before the women arrived in large numbers, the men maintained an understanding that work was not so serious, that work should not overwhelm the pleasant state of camaraderie that the men had taken pains to cultivate. sometimes men lounged around the water coolers telling jokes to one another. sometimes lunches were prolonged. sometimes their lunches included manhattans or martinis.

when the women were permitted, the work became more serious. during the war, which was serious, the women worked. after the baby boom, the women, who had been sent back to their kitchens after the men returned from war, wanted to be permitted even though they had no war to permit them. they had more to prove. they had to be serious. when they entered the workplace they picked up the pace. and most of the men stopped launching paper airplanes from their desks.

which may have been the reason my mother tried to warn me.

but I wanted to work because I thought work was the place where the world's serious people conducted the world's serious business.

mothers were not the serious part of life. at home was not the important place. few played house at the serious office.

You're writing a book? they inquire.

Yes.

About?

Work, I tell them, biting the left side of my mouth.

Work? they laugh, like how could anyone in their right mind.

An exposé? Eyes widening.

No, experimental lyric prose, I tell them. Disappointing perhaps, it not being an exposé and all, but they don't let on.

Am I in it? asks Joan, the secretary with the yellow beads.

Am I? asks Joyce.

What about us?

Well, I hedge, beginning to explain that it's not quite like that either.

Hey, make me thinner will you, Joan urges.

The new one with stiletto heels snorts: Yeah, make me smarter.

I want red hair, says the one with grey.

Taller, much taller.

Anything else? I ask the group, who giggle with the possibilities.

Yeah, make me rich.

Me too. Me too. The corridor filling up with giggles.

Can't wait to read it, says Julie, the shortest. Especially the part where I'm five eleven. Hey, why not six one.

After that always: How's the novel? Finished yet? Don't forget the red hair, with a sweep of her hand curving back from her forehead, demonstrating the luxurious length and volume of her auburn request.

Me, always a little nervous, a little proud.

I go to the bank. Money leaves the bank. Despite my vigilance, consumed.
Consuming: note pads and running shoes and reading glasses   gasoline
and a string of pearls   organic ginger tea   HB pencils and ornate picture
frames sushi   60 watt bulbs   bottled water and silver earrings   Anacin
                I am what I consume
                     what consumes me
        how I spend my time   my money
            the ginger tea's organic   the picture frames are gold

      work results in heat and ashes
    how will I be if I leave
                mission statements having consumed me   program
plans and outcome goals having ground down my time   I've given up on
outcome for myself
        adrift as a mariner

          who will recognize me
             without my albatross
  this was never my intention
I only wanted to pay the rent
            make the world a fairer place

  yet now   am spent   this work is spending me

My belly full of days

And in my mind the whirr of teeth

That first day in the Grade Four classroom of St. Joseph's school, I was a foreigner. Waiting for the codes to gel, for the Catholic smells to fade into the background. For the short hand to reach the 3.

Miss Gilhooley made me stay past the 3 to write out the Apostle's Creed. From memory. The other girls left. Staying after school was supposed to stimulate my memory. I wondered how to contact my mother. Tell her not to wait dinner. I had no memory of an Apostle's Creed. No chance of ever leaving this strange basement classroom. I sat at my foreign desk with the lift-up top in the Catholic classroom on my first day with a lined sheet of yellow paper. The short hand on the 4. I bit the soft skin inside my cheeks. Even though my mother warned me.

Leave it on my desk when you finish, Miss Gilhooley said over her shoulder, as she left for the teachers' room. She needed a cigarette.

Then Colleen, a short girl with a round face, who had volunteered to clean Miss Gilhooley's blackboards, to wash their chalky surface with a wet sponge in long downward strokes, began a loud whisper, keeping her eyes focused on the wet blackboard: I believe in God the Father. . . .

"Some scientists have warned of information overload as office workers
live virtual existences, sending and receiving up to 150 (e-mail)
messages a day." (http://www.sunday-times.co.uk/news/pages/
sti/2001/03/04/stiwenews 01034.html)

Scientists . . . warn . . . office workers
                live virtual.

            One virtual day at a time.
            Virtual alarms.
            Crunching processed cereal with almost milk. 1%.
            Chugging decaf coffee with Sweet 'NLow.
            Putting one virtual foot in front of the other.
            Out of the morning house into the still-dark car.
            The morning virtual, more like night.
            Alone. Breathe the virtual high-octane air.

Part Three
FASTER

Tuesday 8:28 — Prepare another report on housing program, including current stats, up-to-date evaluations, rationales for program planning at the top. My head on the heel of my hand. My teeth chewing inside my cheeks.

Tuesday 11:00 — Deliver presentation to new Interns with slides and a consumer to answer questions. Wearing my new black suit.

Tuesday 1:00 — Demonstrate usefulness of improvements to the Access System to the Housing Team. Show why these changes matter. Use clearest voice.

Tuesday 3:00 — Attend newly formed Provincial Committee to implement recommendations of the Simpson Commission. Brush the shoulders of my new black suit.

Tuesday 5:15 — Prepare notes to report on Committee progress to the Inter-Regional Implementation Team. Tongue the new hole inside my mouth.

Tuesday 6:00 — Read e-mail regarding budget cuts. Cracking my neck from side to side.

Tuesday 6:30 — Pull budget file. Pack briefcase. Check pocket for Anacin. Flick computer off.

counting again
not days
        but steps from the underground parkade
                        to the elevator
faces around a meeting table
reports on my desk
tiles on the women's bathroom floor
dollars assigned to my outcome plan
gold stars in a scribbler
numbers of e-mail
        every morning on the screen   116 this morning before 8:15

        like beads on a rosary
                like jellybeans in a jar
                        not for eating   just for the contest   the $2 prize
I'm guessing 769 jellybeans 71 rosary beads 116 e-mails

the other side of the 5 dollar bill
always 2 sides
                        at least according to Solomon
                5 sides if you're a pentagon
8 if you're an water spider

time is breath sucked out of me
if I deplane   mid-air
I must start counting   backward   spinning
and counting
if I stop or lose my nerve   or my place in the countdown   I will
faster   panic
never know when
to pull the cord
watch the sky's breath billow silk
in red and gold

Late morning, 9:53. Mid-meeting. 20 of us, no, 17, sit at this polished mahogany table. 20 feet long, curved at both ends though you could hardly call it oval. Stan sits across from me. He's writing too, with a yellow pencil. He leans back, looking through wire-rimmed glasses at the Director of Planning who is speaking. K hunches over the five-page agenda at the far end of the table. He wears no hat; his shoulders bow around his ears. Everyone watches the speaker; no one seems to notice K. The woman next to K asks him a question; he nods but keeps his eyes on the agenda in front of him. The speaker's office is on the top floor. She has something important to say. "We are beginning to look at a number of strategic policy changes for the corporation." She scans the faces around the table, assuring herself that we are listening. "You've received a series of e-mail documents spelling out new executive directions that will maintain our leadership position of excellence. We intend to support strategic, evidence-based service changes that will move us forward in our pursuit of excellence." Stan purses his lips like they're on drawstrings. He glances at me then wrinkles his brow, crossing his arms over his pale green shirt and dark green tie. He has the kind of bald head that makes his scalp look like a pink rubber clown cap. His eyes move from the Director of Planning to the window. I wonder whether he thinks I'm writing about him. He picks up his pencil again. He could be writing about me. I look back to the presenter hoping she will not suddenly interrupt her presentation to single me out: "What are you writing? Bring it to the front of the class. Now!" But her eyes are on K, squinting.

A woman in a black turtleneck and black suit with a large silver pin smiles as the next presenter jokes about his lack of technical ability. Grey shirt, grey pants, grey on the board room walls. Then he explains: "We are not allowed to go into a deficit situation." Five of us writing. "As you know," he continues, "we introduced a mixed financial system with some trepidation." The woman in the black suit drapes her arm over the back of her chair. Her eyes hang heavy-lidded and her hand droops in a graceful curve from her black and silver wrist. Her eyes steady on the speaker. I keep writing.

"Then early in the year we had a shock, a $300,000 deficit." He jokes, of course that's not the only shock we've had this year. Giggles ring around the room. This presenter is well-liked. "On top of that they began to play another game," he says. A long story pivoting on words like deficit and calculation. He fans out information sheets which are "as current as they can be," to establish his credibility. His jokes reveal that others are at fault, but changes are inevitable.

A man in a white shirt sits four along from me. He has a heart condition and has been away recently because of heart surgery. His face is bright pink. He sits with his chin on the knot of his tie, reading the sheets in front of him. Three more start writing. Two whisper. No one likes change. No one likes being told the inevitable.

The presenter clicks on an overhead chart with columns of numbers. It lights up the whole screen, pulled down from the wall, spilling light upward onto the grey ceiling. The secretary in a silk blouse with a frilled collar types the minutes onto her laptop.

Stan has turned around 90 degrees in his seat. Faces front now, chewing along the thumb side of his hand. Gently. Chews his index finger, pulling on the dark hairs that grow on the back of the finger. Behind the presenter's words, the clicking of the laptop, the hum of the overhead projector. My legs ache. Stretching them, I curl my left foot upward, trying not to kick other legs under the table. People scowl, knit their fingers, whisper. The presenter, it turns out, is asking them to take on more work. "Big nuisance factor," says the languorous woman in black and silver. Stan nods, picks up his pencil. Change means more work. Inevitably.

My head is ½ asleep. But only ½. So far. 10:17, the meeting only ½ over.

K eyes me from his end of the table as the woman next to him asks him a question. He topples his leather chair as he rises and it crashes against the wall. Managers lean out of his way as he bustles from the room, banging into Stan on the way out. His chair rests on its back legs.

looking up I see
        my jacket streaming open
dreaming this high-wind parachute
five-petalled   legs spread   arms spread
            on the ground I strain   arms up   to catch my five-petalled
self bigger and then bigger   the offices of gravity
            falling now directly
            heavy as a mantle
            into my reach
missing the painted target
                but landing all the same   crashing
                into me

Catechism homework I did with my father in the evenings, that first year.
My mother shook her head, towel-dried the turnip pot.

What is God? he asked from page one of the thin white and blue
paperback text.

And my answer (THE answer): God is love.   Working toward belief

Page one, question one. Central theological issue: What is God? From
which reasons and the good life flow.
But . . .

And we are his children.
But . . .
                     Only if we work at it. . . .

His beloved and chosen children.
                     Only if we do not dream too much, want to leave.

Later in October when I figured out the system, the Catechism, the cursive script, the tea towel embroidery, I began to get higher marks. Better and better report cards: 85%, 92%. Positioning myself in the top of the class. Not for my mother who disliked the Catholics. Or for my father who was too busy. For myself: I liked the game, the higher numbers. The counting. Up.

counting down is more complicated
        than the straightforward: 3-2-1-zero
                blastoff

                    no walls
             into the stratosphere

        now I understand the sound of fear
            in the concept stratosphere.

        no carpeted corridors with plum-coloured
woodwork, no budget files, no metal filing cabinets with doors that stick,
no clocks on boardroom walls, no mailroom dust finer than silica, no
twice monthly paycheques, or paystubs, no Sandra, Reneé chatting in the
hall, no one to e-mail orders: do this, do that
no end of day, no start, nothing in between

the man in the 16th century would not leave his cell: he understood the fear

Another thing: They ask me to stay
      And I stay
      Squint hard

That and the cash
Status and gold frames
How the world ca-chings round the clock
Call it Monday if you want to
Monday is the same as Wednesday
Wednesday's not unlike the rest

He's here again. It's been awhile. He's sitting at my round little table drumming his fingers and whistling. Head tilted up, leaning back and whistling. Smooth. I haven't seen him light-hearted before. I've been at too many meetings, on the phone too much. When I see him, I flop my briefcase to the floor, step toward him, then realize I don't know him well enough to touch him. I've missed him. I close the door behind me. Always trying to trap him. As if.

I didn't know you could whistle, I say. It doesn't fit your image. Even though it's a lieder tune (though *tune* is overstating it) with long forlorn notes that warble into haunting rhythms. I grab a Kleenex, blow my nose. He stops and clears his throat.

as i recall from our last conversation, you won't be leaving this place, he turns his head toward the window, as you thought you would. i feel somewhat responsible, my books are like that with endings, unpredictable, dreary. a style that bears my name. this non-ending in the middle makes you despondent; i am trying to alleviate your gloom. now that i am writing again, sometimes i almost burst with cheer. let me whistle you a happy tune, the happiness in my tune may convince you that you're not afraid, not alone, perhaps. i can try whistling Dixie. words are not always necessary; they have been overrated, given too much power. but music . . . did your father whistle? it used to be more common.

He tried to teach me, but I never was much good. I blow a breathy rendition of "Zippity Do Da" through my pursed lips, which demonstrates how not much good I was.

This time K fades more slowly. Along with the vibrato of his whistling, he gradually disappears. I want to run into the next office, say come and see. A happening. But I don't even open my door. No one goes by in the few minutes of his fade-out. The phone doesn't ring. Finally only the faintest last notes of "Whistle While You Work." Wistful like a long goodbye down a twilight city lane. Far off, around a curve, past another office building, and another and another.

St. Joseph is the patron saint of work, wearing work-a-day brown robes, hammer in hand on his ecclesiastical marble pedestals. Serviceable, productive: St. Joseph of the workers, wearers of brown, black or grey, navy. But, given his special son, he is not, strangely, the patron saint of fathers. St. Joseph was just an older man standing in for Dad. St. Dad the worker. Who is just a man standing in day-to-day for Santa Claus, the patron saint of toys. Who is a grandfatherly man standing in for Mickey Mouse. Who is a virtual mouse standing in for whatever might be missing. St. Mickey.

Which saint will intercede for me?

Noon. Winds blowing and sunshine. Someday the sunshine will be mine. Staring out my north-facing window, no lunch break today.

The maroon maple leaves flip and twist in the wind, their undersides pink. Waving in the whirl of midday air.

My mother in the house, with the sewing machine for company, my father out of the house with the habit of overwork, neither knew the world I wanted. My belief in a different world.

When I started working my mother said: Why are you working? Stay home with your children.
I said, Women are part of the world. Everything was changing then around me, the TV showed people burning draft cards and effigies and bras. No. They never showed the bras.

Serious, important. I wanted to be in the changing world. Insert my values. She shook her head.

I give people housing. Change their world. A bit. one sq. ft. at a time.   By my latest accounting, I have now improved the world by 200,000 sq. ft. 2 decades of working in special needs housing equals 200,000 sq. ft. of improvement, of new and better housing. Give or take.   400 roofs over > 400 heads.

400 roofs/ > 400 heads = X (where X stands for a better world).

It's not how I expected things to work, but it's how this change happens. Slowly, by my calculations.

my father left the house at 8 AM
when my father left the house
            the house silenced
                        for awhile
a silence that shifted
                    with the sound
                    of a faucet running
                            or the radio
or my mother talking bridge games on the phone

when my mother left
                    the house   the house did not fill up   the curtains did
not billow   the fridge door did not open to release the fridge's light
pots huddled on their shelves   the house
held its breath   for as long
                            as she was gone

I'll work until a door opens.
Collect my pension. Finally.

The work ethic has its own monopoly:
                    Collect $200. Wait another turn. Throw the dice again.

The worst thing about work is not being able to get out.
The cycle round and round.
                    Until a door cracks open.

my father ate his lunch in downtown delicatessens
        or greasy spoons or steak houses
        with names like Chez Paul or Moishe's
        rye bread thick with rose-coloured meat
                        neon-yellow mustard
                        coleslaw   green bread
                        and butter pickles
                        vinegar fries

I never lunched with him   have no real evidence
            sometimes I heard him say the names

I know this:
            when he left the house
        he never took a lunch
                        when he left home
        hands in his pant pockets
                        he only took himself

When my father was sixteen he organized community dances, he loved dancing that much. The dances made him extra money. He loved that too. He danced, made money, never stayed at home.

When he came to North America my father was not prepared for any of the jobs he had to take. Talked his way into them. Sure, he said, I can drive the bakery wagon; I'm good with horses. Learning things the hard way, watching his co-workers at the Crane factory, to see how they made sinks. Pretending to know which pipe fit into which other pipe. Pretending not to be afraid when the horse careened down the icy hill, dragging the bakery wagon with it. Finally talked himself into a job in sales. No sinks to fit. No horses to rein. No icy hills. He could sell soap. Talking was his thing, talking like dancing, making people smile and buy his wax and soap and floor machines.

Gave up dances. Worked from 8 till 8, sometimes on Saturday. He told my mother about his sales. Told her about soap, how it was made, how bubbles were not necessary for cleaning, and about waxes, what kind raised the highest polish, what kind left yellow residue around the edges of a vinyl floor. He showed her how to install the heavy round brush into the base of the silver floor polisher. Plugged it in and danced it round and round our kitchen floor. He talked about floor machines and hand driers and the owner of the company and the owner's wife who chose not to own fur coats. He talked about the other guys who never sold as much as him.

Abandoned his need to kick up his heels. Sold sanitary supplies. Talked to strangers on elevators: have you heard the one about the . . . But. Sometimes when he took his hands from his pockets, they hung lonely by his sides. As though they had been abandoned.

my father brought home: soap   bars & bars of industrial soap
            floorwax commercial soaps an industrial strength floor polisher
            a heart condition
            curses for cars that cut him off on the 2 and 20

my mother brought home: tinned vegetables cube steak   Simplicity
            sewing patterns
            bridge club recipes   cheap socks anything on sale
            a sore on her leg that wouldn't heal
            worries that he'd find the bills

I bring home: pens yellow highlighters recycled paper strategic plans
            outcome goals
            extended health care   a pension plan
            headaches
            a belly full of days

when my father returned at the end of his day
  he sat in his chair at the red kitchen table
  my mother at her counter squeezed another lemon for another
    lemon pie
The Montreal Star curved angel wings in his two hands
  as he read her the article on Abitibi mines then told her the
  argument with his boss
  about the boss's brother how he slammed the door
  how his burning ulcers the traffic jam beyond Lasalle
  bloody this and bloody that his hell's bells
  wings tremulous in his two hands
        and falling

my mother rarely left the house like all the mothers on the street she
knew the price of Steinberg's peas and who had left his wife and where
to find the tape how long mitts took to dry angel food to bake
    my father told her whatever else she'd need to know

Want to learn how to dance? he asks me when I'm 10. Here, stand on my feet. The game of feet dancing. That's it; stand right on top, you can't hurt me. Okay now, he says, taking my right hand in his left. Then he moves his feet. Lift step slide, lift step turn. Carefully. A little stiff.

My sock feet clinging to the tops of his wing tips. I bite my underlip to stay aloft, aligned, my hands grip his upper arms through his shirt sleeves, his biceps tense underneath the light blue cotton. I loosen my grip, not wanting to hurt him. Not wanting to get too close to his skin. Curling my toes into his thin shoelaces. My mother and my sister on the sofa, heads following as my father and I circle, synchronize over the green carpeting in the living room with the picture window. One two three, one two three. My sister giggles. I giggle, wanting, not wanting. This game. This close.

He halts. Now try on your own feet. I slide off the tops of his shoes. Firm on my own two I feel the carpet nubble under my cotton socks. Step step slide, step step slide. He bends a little, holds me around my waist. I feel my stomach pull away, not wanting to be held like this. Wanting to dance my own. Feeling all this down to my cotton soles.

No, follow me! He resists my resistance. Like this, he says. Step step slide. It's just the fox trot, for Christ's sake. Now follow. You're supposed to follow me.

Look, he turns to my mother, your daughter can't follow. You're going to have to learn, he advises me, his voice louder. He abandons me mid-step, plants his feet, his hands on his belted waist. It's simple enough advice.

Here, he says, taking my mother, wheeling her close. He's humming waltz music. There's no music playing. Humming and stepping and leading.

My mother turning in the right places like she's part of him. She knows all his moves.

I plunk myself into my mother's velvet depression on the sofa seat, next to my sister. Our elbows bump; we do not giggle. I keep my head forward as though I'm looking out the picture window, as though I'm not following, but my eyeballs rove after the swirls of my mother and father. I learn to follow and not follow. My father's dance steps. Thinking not following could save me for myself.

Today the 29th e-mail reads: New Policy for Performance Evaluations.
Click on attachment:

1. All Managers Shall Be Evaluated—

As with union contracts, all managers shall now be evaluated annually.   Salary increases shall be based on merit and exemplary performance evaluations. Budget management, leadership, fiscal expedience and financial savings shall be key considerations. Team work is also important.

Scrolling down.

2. All Managers Shall Create Suitable Goals and Objectives—

Personal goals for management careers must be established and reviewed on an annual basis. Department heads must approve all employment goals. Objectives must be consistent with corporate directions, including budget management, leadership, fiscal expedience and financial savings.

This language is another language. I learned it years ago, can even write it, but now can hardly read it.

3. No Manager shall be concerned with endings—

Managers concerned with endings as a personal employment goal will be considered for immediate termination.

Stop!

Who's writing this story?

I leave notes for him in yellow file folders, put them in my out-tray. If he is still writing this story, how will I get to the ending, my final day of this?

Dear ghost-writer: Remember, I am also the narrator. I want to get out, intact, with benefits, and soon.

But what if a door fans open and I don't. What if I don't know how to leave.

home Friday at 6   early
5 days behind me
       closer to what . . .
              but at least those 5 are gone

euphoric for this
       sunslants orange/black on kitchen cabinets,
on her face at the sink

I shout   I clap my hands
so lightened to have arrived
       on this light-filled evening   early
              and 5 more behind me
am too involved in my own noise
       to see how slow she lifts her eyes
       notice what she doesn't say

stock market versus kitchen

fat pig versus fried egg

e-mail versus poem

calendar versus final day

bacon versus everything else

home again home again

briefcase versus girlfriend

don't get enough jiggity jig

The everyday surprise: the day ends. This surprise is a surprise every day. Five o'clock arrives. Then it is 5:15. That's the surprise. Then 5:45. I'm still at my desk. I breathe out.

I used to arrive home from work panting. Tear open the mail. Read the first line. Yank the fridge door. Bite into a radish. Another. Crunch sounds inside my middle ear. Flick on the radio over the fridge. Upstairs. Peel off my bra. Pull on sweat pants. No belts, no buckles. Crashing down the stairs. Circle. Circle. Crashing up the stairs. A dog who's barred from the house. Panting. Yipping and panting. Consuming rooms and stairs, swallowing time before the people notice.

Lately sometimes I just collapse like an ironing board on top of my queen size bed, shoes flexed, arms splayed. That tired. Breathe in, breathe out. Shallow. No desire inside any cell. No interest in radishes or the radio or colliding through the diagonal air of home. Not opening the mail, reading the first line. Not unsnapping my bra. All the panting stuck below my throat.

When my father strode into the house he emptied his pockets onto the corner of the counter that was his. The tall white side of the fridge forming a wall for his day's leavings. In the morning he always left some paper scraps inside that square foot of counter to protect his claim. At the end of the day his thick hands scooping the clutter from his pant pockets: pennies, Chiclets, keys, Export A's, matchbooks, toothpicks, more paper scraps. Turning his hands over, palms down, in a final gesture. The clatter of the landing, loud as a midway in our small kitchen.

I am morphing into something else with scraps of paper, stubs of pencils. Confiding on the page in secret. Scratching onto paper. Memo poems. Notations to myself. Mapping a way out.

The word 'metamorphosis' comes to mind but it's too catastrophic, a man turning into a man-sized insect, mythological, almost cliché.

how make a poem from this
fast-paced mess of a long-gone so-called 9 to 5
& up at 6 or 10 to 6 a regimen
of back-to-back-to-back
must not forget to breathe   fast
fast-framed life of work-a-day into night
awake at 3 AM   panic state
remembering I should make that call
tell my assistant: send the contract
and by the way where is that file

then quick I tuck my pillow   sink my head
6 o'clock bombards too soon
blasts news that's hardly new

is there a story sleeping here

how rise above   fall out of bed   again and everyday
keep mind on meeting schedules   while soaping in the shower
trying to remember   what was important to recall
a file maybe or a contract start
and all this the same for days and weeks and months ahead
metered in scraps of disappearing
time me rocketing along this freaked-out
                                        streak of space
legs rotating like some kid cartoon
heart knocking knock knocking at the bone-barred wall
dancing with the traffic lights
phone on gooley gooley
tea bag stewing in the cup

how find   how shape
a poem from that

by noon the humming starts
along the shoulder ridge down arms
so loud it dins my ears   by 3 PM
my feet don't touch the mauve-flecked floors
& wings speed-beat around my eyes
by 6   by 6 PM   how smooth soothe
the shrapnel of whatever's left
how make a poem from all that roiling pace
spinning silver beads
how see feel shape
how
how word
        a string of pearls   from this

The lunchroom odour of tomato soup slithers up my nostrils, the smell of the Benedict Labre House soup kitchen, that old poverty smell. But these are administrative headquarters. The lunchroom. It's just tomato soup.

Sunlight melts through the south-facing window-wall, glides hot butter over the tables. Three managers perch on the edges of plastic chairs near the window, as though waiting for the start of a race. One, a new one from another location, examines her white knuckles. The other two, Jean and Bianca, grip coffee cups and tête-a-tête in whispers, their shoulders almost touching. Kafka's thin navy back hunches alone at a table near the stove. I join him, but as I tuck in my chair he checks his pocket-watch, reviews the room in a back and forth swivel of his head, scrapes his chair backward and evaporates. The manager with the white knuckles tilts her head in my direction, scowls, returns to her knuckles. I eyeball each person. No one looks about to scream. I pull back the top of my low-fat blueberry yogurt.

The secretaries are playing lunch, setting out their sandwiches at the largest vinyl-topped table, pulling dishes from microwaves, adding salt to bowls of soup. This one hour of escape. Talking and talking. About eating, work, escape. Eating and talking: That's my tuna submarine on the second shelf. . . .

Supposed to be humid today; not so humid you can't breathe . . . lucky the air conditioning is working again.

Lived in Texas, my skin was awful . . . in the offices, all that paper . . . In Cuba after a week my skin was lush.

Ice storm in Ottawa last week   Government worker broke his neck leaving work. . . .

Now they're over 90 degrees!   Springtime in Ontario!

You hear? They're moving the Contract Department to the Larch Building; they'll all have to go.

Why do that, cost a bundle and they'll move 'em back next year.

Their cymbaline laughter, heads arched back, mouths open.

High heels click into the lunchroom. The three managers brush their laps, rise, leave.

Marilyn, with yellow beads around her neck, approaches the long table carrying a basket of cranberry scones leftover from a meeting to celebrate John's retirement. With tiny packets of butter and jam and cream cheese. A new woman eating soup, takes a scone to go with her soup, which, she advises, is low-cal, the soup, not the scone.

What is it on Atkins, the secretary with the lush skin asks, proteins, grapefruits?

No, the woman with the soup says, anything but carbs. You don't worry about fats. Fortunately, she adds, I don't like fats. My parents had to remove all fats from my plate. Her security card hangs around her neck from a long black lace with yellow happy faces stamped along its length. She steadies the card at her breast as she leans in for another spoonful of her low-cal soup.

My computer was down this morning. Can you believe? Computer support line, busy for ages. They expect us to work like that?

Another virus is what I heard.

Burnt toast's bitter incense circles among us. Tin foil rustles.

What's COWER stand for? Three of them take turns guessing.
That's it, says Joan: Committee of Work Evaluation Ready, plucking burnt
toast from the toast. It's in my acronym file.

Come on Joan, you made that up. An acronym file!

Gas station on the corner's gone. Over the weekend. Totally. Giant hole in
the ground.

So fast; like it was never there.

Angie picks up spinach pie in her long-nailed fingers. Chewing, chewing,
rubbing her finger tips together, hand high over her paper plate. Filo flakes
fall, a light snow, from her burgundy nails.

Where'd you get the pie? I ask her from my table. I hardly ever take a
lunchroom lunch.

New Greek place, where that sushi take-out used to be.

Hey, that's cold air blowing on my head, complains the high-heeled woman,
just started in Finance, clerical. I'd rather be out in that sun. Don't you wish
you had the day off, she asks, more to herself than to the rest of us. We
synchronize our heads in her direction. She shrugs her shoulders.

Yeah, wish I was back in Cuba.

Yeah, with Tom Hanks.

Oh great! We're wishing our lives away, says Joan, looking up from her *Chatelaine*. Isn't that awful?

I rarely use the lunchroom.

Some never do; eat lunch at their desks everyday.
Desk-food in their offices, or in their cubicles. Cubicle food: muffins, take-out sushi, yogurt, sticks of celery, apples. One-handed food.

Others leave the building. Errands or air. Eat in cafés or in their car, egg-sandwiched hands balanced on the driver's wheel.

In the summer, the lunchroom rests vast and unpeopled, tables wait, but no one comes. In the summer even desk-eaters sometimes leave the building, push open front doors, look for the sun.

red-berry me   carmine
        my mouth   my eyes
                scarlet all my skin to shine

I am the round vermillion
        ringing in the trees
                babies' breasts
        tangerine alveoli   breathing storms
within this pomegranate cavity
                a Chinese painting
                        flying at my eyes
all oppositions
        solved in red and green

                burn chair   desk   all record
        of my lives
                        while offices
                        to ashes

release
cluster me
        against sheen
            & leafy shadow

                noon   this time
                    I cannot stop the blaze

just before one o'clock I swallow summer heat
prod my feet from park to office building
sign myself in
deep inside the high-rise moving up

Later in the afternoon when I return from a meeting to my new office on the south side, a thank-you card decorated with forget-me-nots perches on my desk. From Claire, the secretary I just hired, temporarily, to replace, again, Nina, who is now on stress leave. Thanks for hiring me, in round, blue writing.

The message arrow flashes red on the phone. I've abandoned my desk too long. Outside my new south-facing office window, two stories down, two men with a grocery cart open the blue dumpster lid and peer in. Bulging white plastic bags swing from their arms. A length of coiling razor wire mounted on a cement wall behind them protects the apartment building across the lane from the men with the plastic bags, and from the night.

Edgy, says a manager from the north side of the building, popping her head in to check out my new office. I kind of like it, all that razor wire; view's kind of New York, she says.

Kind of fitting, is what I call it.

Changes in this organization began two years ago with talk of mergers. Which led to the amalgamation of three hospitals and four community agencies last year. This year changes multiply, explode, circle us like recycled office air. No one can ignore it. Mergers merge and morph again. Two more agencies join the core, like adding to a ball of string. One hospital reneges and leaves the core. Organizational names rise and pass. A new logo appears on letterhead, tilting-heart-in-pink-and-blue. Old logo, purple-green-spinning-tree, is discarded. The secretaries gather all old letterhead, send it away to be shredded. New letterhead arrives in boxes.

The Communications Director leaves for the private sector. Three Premises Managers, four Co-Ordinators and a Facility Manager retire early. New secretaries, on contract from temp agencies, perch in the abandoned ergo-chairs of former secretaries, on sick leave or stress leave.

The organization, like a small unstable state run by a mad dictator, shifts a third time. Cuts and fiscals slide sideways. Harder and harder to track the players, dates, reasons, scope. Harder to care. No one has seen old Bill for weeks. Rumours say Doreen was moved to another Regional.

As if volume of work was not enough, now unpredictable transformation. Exhausting to the point of giddy. New security passes for the parkade. Another coffee machine—it won't take quarters. New policies on reporting structures. A second budget request form. To be stapled to the first and signed by superiors no one knows.

My father's old saying: a change is as good as a rest. From another time entirely, before change became a hyper-active digital-cartoon character, legs rocketing beneath its animated robot body.

How much change = how much rest? Whatever the answer, I feel comatose.

126

The molecules of his shrinking physique undulate now in a spirited way, so that I have trouble keeping him solid before my eyes. He stands now no more than 4 feet. Haven't noticed this reduction before. So thin when he turns sideways I almost want to cry. He blurs along his edges. I squint hard to keep him in focus. He doesn't make it easy. But things weren't easy for him: his father, his writing, his difficulty sleeping, his difficulty eating.

So much is changing, I say, the office reallocations, the staff cuts, the phone numbers, that I wondered if you'd find me.

inevitable, he replies. there is only one speed now and that is faster. who wrote that? He tilts his head. when they start to move this fast, you must speed up, speed up your plans as well.

Plans? Plans have disappointed me since my countdown failed. Right now you're my only plan despite how thin you're wearing.

disappointment must not be indulged, he tells me, his little hand slapping my round table top. it leads to self-pity, which is helpless. i plot the only way i know, harder as the end encroaches. he removes his bowler hat, scratches his dark head. authorities seek me now throughout this edifice. are you aware? His head swivels as he shoulder-checks the room. have you noticed cameras, microphones, disturbances and signs of traps? in your office? security roams the parkade, these corridors. i have reduced my size, this is how i manage, through metamorphosis. i change my breathing tempo. and writing of course; i always manage if i write. lifting a hand to his shrunken mouth, he coughs. have you located the first part of my manuscript yet? he coughs again. he chokes. i left it at the start before you started writing.

Where?

in your other office, before we met. you are still writing, i hope, still purposeful about escape?

I can't look at him. There's always something out of synch, I tell him. For instance, I now fit in better than I thought. I notice my successes. I count my friendships, passing the same people in the same halls for years. Smiles happen. I would miss them. At the same time, I still hold this tightness at the base of my throat. I never see my honey. I'm in a kind of limbo. But, if I leave, how would I see you?

careful, he scowls.

Terence, the new inhabitant of my former office, leaves the building at 5:45 that night. I revisit my old north-side space, nod to the maple tree, its branches bare outside the window, pick through desk papers in search of K's manuscript. Before I rummage through the drawers and leaf through binders on the shelves, I check the bookcase shelves. I check behind the bookcase. I lean my shoulder into its pressed-board side, grunt and shove, shove and grunt. Inch by inch I ease the seven-foot structure, binders shifting and tilting above my head, notepads plummeting, away from the wall. A swish sound close to my ear stops silent at the carpet, and there it is, curled and splayed against the wall. I straighten its curls inside one of Terence's empty yellow folders, check the corridor, click his door shut and scuttle back to my new office overlooking the razor wire.

After reading it at my desk, the beginning, no end, I lean into my elbows and eye the lonesome dumpsters below. Lights across the lane yellow the apartment windows. My phone rings, I pick up, no one speaks. I count my fingers, pull my earlobes, pack my briefcase, go home.

Wait for her to get home too. Union meeting.

Examine the mail: flyers, bills, deals, questionnaires.

128

7:45 sizzle lamburgers for dinner, on English muffins, Dijon.
Remember two items for tomorrow's AM meeting. Jot
   them down.
Sonicare my teeth. Slip into bed.   Early. Wait for her.
Dream of caymans from the story of Frances K.

* * *

No one keeps records of this change. No one chronicles the history of the
shrinking budgets in Programs and the growing budgets in Public Relations.
No one counts which positions have been terminated. No one records the
reasons why. Or why in the next year the terminated positions are added
once again but with different titles. No one evaluates the switches. No one
researches whether or not it's more useful to have Finance on the fourth
floor of 982 Ashbury or the sixth floor of 1209 Rowan. Change being
next to godliness.   But I keep an archive in my mind, notice that:

1.   Our Executive Director sends an e-mail in May, regretting to
      inform us of his resignation. His successor sends an e-mail
      early December, regretting same. Still, months later, no one
      takes his place. Not yet.

2.   The corporation's name cannot settle down on letterhead or on
      signs. Public Relations adds a word, then removes it and adds
      two more. Health this, Health that and that. Staff call it what
      we want.

3.   Now I report to Housing, not Mental Health. New boss.

4.   I move to a back office along a dreary corridor, so I can sit in
      the Housing Dept. I miss my mountain view.

5.   The Chevron Station two blocks away vanishes into a pit
      in the ground. Big hole. I wonder what happened to Steve,
      who used to wash my windscreen, complain about global
      warming.

6. Vanity Dry Cleaning jacks up the price of cleaning my two piece suits.

7. Titles too: Director This is now Manager That. Manager This is now Coordinator That.

8. Governments swing right, left, then right again; our budgets swing right, left, then cut some more.

9. Whole new departments spring from the Zeus-like heads Executives. Departments blend. No one talks to anybody, like dysfunctional families.

10. *Right-sizing* replaces the word *downsizing*, which sounds too much like jobs were being cut. Accurate, but the word has 'down' right in it.

11. New and newer policies to keep up with zigzagging corporate directions.

12. Managers move staff to different offices in different buildings across town, and then return the same staff to their original offices, like a new board game they got for Christmas, called "Office".

13. My assistant goes home with headaches and shoulder pain. She never comes back. New secretaries arrive every month from the Girl Friday Agency. Every month, another secretary. I lose track of their names.

14. Service boundaries waver: old district maps came down, borders are redrawn. Once, twice, three times. Another kind of board game.

15. Someone stacks 17 more boxes in the back corridor one week, then 22, then 36. The boxes tower and totter against the north wall.

16. My calculated monthly pension amount shrinks like a desiccating sponge. By their calculations.

17. My face grooves eight new wrinkles around my mouth and

eyes, and one on each earlobe.

18. Seasons change: cool swings warm, warm swings cool again, then rain, then hail.

19. Kafka shrinks. He's thinner, shorter now.

I'm still here

This change streams like the smell of burnt coffee through our offices. This change accounts to no one, drifts storms of papers onto our desks.

I need a rest; this change is not.

My father lived in his own time. He wore a fedora. He didn't own a briefcase. He didn't wear a watch. He rushed around in his own directions. His time was human-sized, male-sized at the time. Some nights when he finally got home he threw his pocket change onto the counter like he was throwing Jacks. Maybe he needed rest too.

punch in 5-2-6-1 to kill alarm
toss keys on bookshelf
coat on hanger   scarf on hook
briefcase on stairs
mail on kitchen table
jacket on chair
Lean Cuisine in microwave

flick on the lights

7 on Friday   sky's plunged blue black
she's away   radio's reporting bombings in Chechnya
nobody's home
can't stop the hum

Part Four
THROUGH THE LOOPHOLE

New corporate memos on my computer screen every day, every half day.
    One memo begins:
    We are moving forward (and I thought we were moving in
    all directions at once) in a cultural shift toward continuing
    advancement developing a dynamic work environment (someone
    has to write this—must be Jean) with proactive and visionary
    leadership which emphasizes renewal, choice (theirs, not mine)
    and flexibility (ours, not theirs) to motivate (sic) us in our
    progressive employer (fee fie foe fum) and employee relationships
    and our continuing pursuit of excellence.

Another foundational memo. It says: Believe. It says nothing else. I
smell the continuing pursuit of progressive Apple Pie in those complex,
flavoured words. Without any scent of meaning.

        The memo ends:
        Those staff who wish to pursue the details of these
        changes, can access our staff-only Change Website at
        www.mustchangenow@ improve.com.

Who has the time? Or the interest? Maybe Rita. She likes acronyms.
Maybe Bill, he loves the Internet. Maybe someone who wants a laugh at
4:15 with tea?

        Old orders change, giving way to more orders.

Belief is foundational. So is disbelief.

How will I care for my disbelief when disbelief is so hard to hold, a cayman with a head full of teeth?

These corridors with plum-coloured pile and drywall painted pearly grey, narrow as my spread palms, this is the place I've wandered my adult life. This is where I am this kind of me, acceptable me, the me who dresses in dark suits and silver, the me who says, add this to the agenda for next Monday's meeting, the me who decides which program gets which money. The world goes round and round, nods its head, approves of me this way.

Living this blend of high-octane adrenalin, caffeine and Anacin, how can I stop long enough to write my resignation letter, rise from my padded ergo-chair, depart without my yawning briefcase, into a simpler life of camomile tea (without need for caffeine) and hard biscuits (without need for treats) and drift like a maple leaf, floating, falling, nothing in my hands.

When the countdown ran out, and organizational change seeped under every office door, I began to sense, more than know. Like approaching thunder, or a rainbow coalescing, the ozone changed. Amped up. Pins loosened. Time became liminal. A yellow folder, open to the end, lying on my ergo-chair. More Frances Keegan from Franz Kafka.

* * *

Well. I am afraid, Ms. Keegan—Doctor Frame did not call her Frances—I'm afraid that I am stumped. He leaned forward across his black lacquered desk and whispered: I have no explanation. The desk a square black pond, nothing but reflections on its surface. He leaned back in his swivel chair, inserted his baby finger into his right ear and shook it. He withdrew the digit and inspected the tip. No explanation, that is, for your "condition," he said. He crooked his index fingers to indicate quotation marks around the word "condition."

There has to be an explanation, Frances said. I don't have time for this sort of thing.

Well, Ms. Keegan, this is highly unusual. A new strain of leprosy perhaps? He scratched the top of his white head. But I doubt it. He pursed his pink lips and rolled his eyes. It is fortunate you do not suffer any pain; you may have to wait months before you see the specialist. He rose to see her out. My secretary will call you. He held the office door open for her and watched as she replaced her baby finger, her molars, her earlobes, and another finger into the Ziploc bag.

Frances resolved to keep her condition from her parents. This required subterfuge. But she'd worked in bureaucracy for many years and had risen steadily in the organization, so she was no stranger to the concept. Despite losing additional toenails and her middle right toe, she distracted her parents with descriptions of the 24/7 moat construction. The construction company used klieg lights through the night. When it was finished the moat would be ten feet deep and five feet wide. There would be two drawbridges with computerized lifts and pulleys.

Yes, with alligators, she told Gregor one Wednesday morning during a phone call to the semi-desert where he studied insects and slept in a tent.

Unnatural, said Gregor.

Speaking of unnatural, Frances wanted to tell him about her missing fingers and toe, I've been having some trouble myself.

Your parents? Gregor said. They need to get their own place. I can't believe—

It's my hand, she said.

Your singing's coming along, he said.

Thanks, she said, but my hand. And now my foot.

That lieder music is kind of unnatural itself, he said.

No, it's romantic.

You just miss me, said Gregor.

Finally, one Monday at dinner Frances reported the arrival of the reptiles. *Ludicrous!* said her mother. *How can they expect alligators to stop that awful music? Waste of money.* Her father nodded without lifting his head from his beef stew. Neither of them asked Frances how she was managing her crocodilophobia.

Not alligators though, said Frances. Caymans. Cheaper. Rumour has it they're from the sewers of New York. Twenty-five caymans. All white. Her father looked up from his stew. Apparently they're blind, she said.

That night she dreamed of Captain Hook. He was looking for his hand. He kept saying: Send up an alarm, you'll have to act your age.

One afternoon in the lunchroom, Shelley (Frances thought her name might be Shelley) asked Frances what her husband did for a living. New, thought Frances. Doesn't know who's management and who's not. Doesn't know she shouldn't be talking to me as though I have time to talk.

Doctoral studies, said Frances. She brushed the shoulder of her black wool jacket. He studies beetles.

THE Beatles, said Shelley, as in John Lennon?

No. Frances couldn't believe she was having this conversation. She shook Sweet 'N Low into her coffee.

As in Volkswagens?

As in dung, said Frances. Dung beetles in New Mexico. She put the cream back in the fridge and strode from the lunchroom.

For weeks Frances avoided the building's main drawbridge. She made a point of driving her car across the rear drawbridge off the lane and into the underground parkade.

Though the mystery music was loudest in the parkade, it was not as unnerving as parking in the adjacent lot and walking over the main drawbridge, over the moat filled with the caymans.

Her assistant told her that when she crossed the main drawbridge in the morning she could see the caymans' shadowy snouts as they lazed in the water. She told Frances that one of the maintenance staff threw in parts of his ham sandwiches on sunny days just to see their mouths snap open and closed. Every morning her assistant told Frances another story. She told her someone had once seen a cayman eat a whole crow. Frances doubted that. She told Frances that some of the reptiles had escaped somehow. Rumour had it that the cayman count was down. Security has covered the moat with a wire mesh screen, said her assistant. They locked it into place at two foot intervals. No one had thought the caymans could escape from a ten foot depth.

Her assistant told her that a white cayman had been found floating belly up in the Burrard Inlet. She said someone had seen a cayman in the ladies' room on the first floor.

The local weekly reported that the caymans were responsible for the underground music. The paper issued an apology the following week.

One Wednesday, Frances took an out-of-town colleague to lunch at a nearby restaurant on West Broadway. It was a sunny day, so they walked. Deep in conversation, they returned via the front drawbridge. A group of five animal rights activists patrolled the front entrance that particular afternoon. They carried signs that read: Caymans Have Feelings Too and Free the Caymans.

On the eastern corner of the moat, the animal care staff, in orange overalls that read Animal Care Staff, placed two large pails on the stonework at the edge of the moat. One of the staff unlocked the security screen and peeled back the mesh. He slopped the contents of the pails into the water. It looked like pieces of white fish. The water around the slops churned with reptile mouths and slapping tails. Frances rushed across the moat followed by her guest and two of the animal rights protesters. She thought she was going to throw up. The two protesters followed Frances and her guest into the elevator.

Management pig-dog. It's worse than a zoo, they said to her as the elevator doors closed. A din of brass and drums started up in the small space as Frances pushed the up button. She left the activists at fourth floor reception, saw Sandra reach for the security phone underneath her counter.

The overwork, the relentless underground music, the continuing office thefts and the moat exhausted Frances. She rarely slept anymore. Other colleagues also confessed to poor sleep and some took prolonged sick leave. The organization hired a clairvoyant.

Frances found herself looking forward to the various tunes, especially the more somber ones and sometimes she hummed along. She admitted to a colleague that she was beginning to enjoy the music mainly in the morning which was her worst time of day. She hoped the clairvoyant would not solve the music mystery too quickly.

A week before Gregor was to arrive home from his first three months in New Mexico, Frances received a call from Finance on the fifth floor. Frances told her assistant to pull the goodwill Works file and bring it up to Max Horton's office.

Frances pushed the button for the elevator. She waited, and when she had counted one hundred and twenty seconds, she decided to take the stairs. She didn't get enough exercise anyway. But as she walked away, the elevator dinged. She turned back, the bronze doors slid open and she stepped on. Three large, buttoned-up managers from another floor crowded the middle space inside. She smiled at them as she pressed five. They were going down. Late lunch, one of them explained. On the main floor they filed off and left her alone to proceed to the fifth. She leaned back against one mirrored wall and watched herself sigh in the mirrored wall opposite her. Multiple reflections into infinity. She hated to see herself sigh. She shifted her weight, squared her shoulders and sucked in her tummy. Her high heel squashed against something in the corner. The something moved, slithered up against her nyloned ankle. She knew what it was before she looked down.

She leapt to the front of the elevator and pressed emergency. Bells rang, the elevator jerked to a halt, and the elevator doors opened short of the fifth floor by about two and a half feet. Frances flung herself over the threshold and half swam, half slid out of the elevator. She lost her shoes. The ring finger on her right hand flew off, her black pearl ring still in place at the base of the finger. Her assistant stepped off the adjacent elevator as

Frances landed. She almost stepped on the finger.

Before Gregor arrived home from New Mexico, Frances submitted her letter of resignation along with a lawyer's letter seeking compensation, 'not only for the accident', the letter read, 'but also for my inability, under the current circumstance, to continue in my chosen career'. Her lawyer assured her that she would have a wealth of public sympathy if she went to the media. She liked the idea of a wealth of public sympathy. He told her that no one ever thought the caymans were a good idea. She said she would think about it; she'd have more time for music. He rubbed his hands together: her compensation could be extremely high, he told her. He looked forward to putting the case together. Very much, he said, and shook her hand. Her absent ring finger tingled as he squeezed her hand; she liked to think it was growing back.

F. K.

* * *

He's perched on my desk at 7 the next morning. Balanced on top of a stack of reports, his legs crossed, feet swinging.

well, he asks before i can get my coat off, how did you like it? such a happy ending.

I look at him over my shoulder as I hang up my jacket. His face smiling the eager question.

Oh Franz, I glance again to check his response; I've never called him Franz before. Don't take this personally, but I found it kind of freakish. I can't use it as a template or even inspiration for my leaving. Did you really think I'd like it?   It resolves nothing.

freakish! he pales paler than usual. it is not freakish, as you say; it is simply what is. you don't see it! any writing that does not hit like a blow on the head is not worth reading. my writing must be like a blow on the head.

Though I feel as though I have been struck, I say to him: I'd have preferred a smoother exit. Caymans! Besides, you used your own initials and your own family circumstances. I haven't lived with my parents for years.

frances keegan is an obvious irish name, even catholic, which was difficult for me. i hope you can understand. at great effort i have done what you have requested. updated my writing style, though max would not approve. researched and rewrote. chose more modern active verbs. and now you tell me you do not appreciate the end i have provided for you. coughing, he extends his hand. please, return the manuscript. i have my admirers still after all these years, perhaps in greater numbers than ever, even if you no longer count among them.

I hand him the yellow folder.

rain all day   that wet sound of end-of-week traffic washing over the Cambie
Street Bridge near our First Avenue office building   that shushing noise
filling the ears like drowning

last night I dreamed they took away my desk. left me a dressing table, paint chipped white and lemony yellow. one day I'll come in and find my desk gone and in its place, that dressing table. one day I'll walk in and forget how to speak. my lips refusing to move. will this fear be held against me too, even if it doesn't happen, just because I dream it?

one day you know you are good at your job, better maybe than anyone else could be, the regular practice of anything improving anything.   it falls on you like a mantle, this knowing, all of a sudden after years.   you know which decisions to approve, which to oppose. when to smile at the new receptionist, when not.   when to remind Records to send a file. know how to calculate the cost of any housing program simple as the cost of oranges in December.   know who to phone when reports are late in March.   when to withhold money.   when to change directions in a meeting. a certain buoyancy resulting (along with and not dispersing the regular and incremental layering of headaches and palpitations and stress, murmurous as tissue paper, the bowing of your shoulders, the humming hunching weight).   close as epidermis.   you have power. you control the work of others.   you win awards. speak at conferences.   but still . . . your activities are of consequence.   you live here most days.   your name is on the door. but . . . they smile when they see you coming, laugh at your jokes.   all this is genuine.   pleasing.   but . . .

. . . still, murmurous as tissue, you want to leave.

still you think
        you want to
                leave.

146

the steady whirr of the building's air-control machinery surrounds me.

they even control the air.

some days I breathe so shallow, at the end of the day I vibrate like a

hummingbird.

my countdown is gone, Kafka is gone, my resolve is going, my only plan now is to write myself out. I write at meetings, my pad below the meeting table in my lap. I write between phone calls on yellow stick 'ems. I write in my car against the middle of the steering wheel driving with my elbows, and on scraps of paper in the middle of the night I write in the dark, not sure in the morning what the wobbly letters mean. I write in the copy room while the Xerox machine makes a dozen copies of the agenda for the next meeting. But. What I notice is that as much as I write myself out, at the same time, I write myself in, deeper, in a way that I had not been in before. Dangerous, attaching myself through writing, making me more here, while more not here.

I pay attention to the details, to the colour of the walls, the plum of the woodwork, the pale yellow of the bathroom stalls, and the colours sneak inside me. I had a way of deflecting the colours of the office before. Paying attention only to the work, to what happens in my mind, the surface, unbelieving, the thin realness of the workplace stayed outside. I never noticed the realness sneaking up on my pink heart, dropping down below my mind's radar, below the wrongs and the overarching weight of work. Have noticed yellow beads. Have noticed maroon leaves shining satin on the tree marooned in the cement of the sidewalk below, the tree which grew thoughtfully to the height of my second story office window simply to make me lift my eyes.

then I left it.

more aware now of what constitutes betrayal.

I elbow the up-button, my arms spilling budget sheets. Rock from left to right. Point my eyes at the elevator doors, willing them to slip open. Three minutes loop by.   I crack my neck, from left to right and read a health poster on the bulletin board beside the elevator: breathe, it tells me. There's nothing else to do; I breathe.   In . . . out . . . in . . .   My stomach inches down and out. I drag up another breath, my feet astride.   Slower. What's the problem: I'm warm, I'm comfortable.   It's not so bad. I almost relax, now only waiting for the elevator. The brushed finish of the elevator doors, breathing. Slide open.

work has started to fit into me,

am now the shape of this job. feel it's unwieldy weight
inside my arms. straighten its pointed collar. brush lint off its broad
shoulders, polish its shoes. I am down shining its shoes when I notice
how much I am looking into the reflection of my job. buffing the surface,
my own shape inside that shine. every minute that happens now happens
between me and this job, this work shape, with hands and a wrist watch,
which is a kind of me, but bigger.

now that I have moved my office I look out my back lane
window and notice: the razor wire, the dumpster, the concrete wall, but
nothing is the maple tree.   how much I miss its leaves.

the rooms of my house   contain
no million dollar budgets   no confidential yellow files   no secretaries in
the hallways
only everydayness lives in my house
        no million dollar budgets   no yellow folders   no staff around the
kitchen table in the rooms of my house   only me and her   a growing
absence growing in between and the sofa   and the fridge   the sink   the
gold frames on the wall somewhere else the consequential   meaning   the
work which fills things up

how can i let go my days at work
        leave one day without my briefcase   close my office door

        which sparrow does not return to the underground parkade
        which dung beetle seeks to shed its festooned shell
        which tree maroons its purpled leaves
        the habit and function of burden
        despite the season, despite the light and lightness of release

the corporation puffs up, merger after merger, while workers are deflated. staff leave, their positions stay like ghosts, not filled. my pants bag around my bottom, my jackets sag from my shoulders. lunch hours become lunch minutes. we are incorporated, *united, formed into one body*, from the Latin: *incorporare*, from the Latin: *corpus-oris* body. but we are disembodied, sized down, submerged. we walk into the lunchroom and see no one. we walk into the ladies'and see no one in the mirrors. no one combs or pats her hair, tubes coral on her lips, checks her teeth. no time. no one nods hello. we wear black, though in more hopeful summer, beige.

two more secretaries move into the office beside me. which makes three in one room. they baffle-board the space between the desks. the new Manager of Communications works in the supply room, her back to me as I grab another pencil and a steno pad.

when the mergers started, it was called amalgamation. nothing would be lost they said: the 'bigger equals better' equation.

the secretary with the yellow beads around her neck shook her head but said: you never know.
knowing but hoping. work is hard enough.

some are told to leave. downsizing. or right-sizing. shakes it all up. even the language downsized, the meanings shrink. *excellence* used to mean *especially* good, now it's just another adjective in a string of hyperbole, *progressive, dynamic, visionary*, gone flat.

before the year was over the second merger struck: bigger than the first, so better. this time no one said you never know. all planning and progress on hold until systems could be harmonized. as if.

Business gurus call the theory Chaos. I should have read the book but there was no time. This chaos kind of change happens like a series of natural disasters. No one keeping up. New faces erupt every week up and down the corridors. Thrown up like folds inside subduction zones. As I become familiar with the face of the new brunette with heavy-rimmed glasses, she leaves. I never knew her name. New people enter and leave. No names. Staff scuttle from their offices for coffee and meetings only. No more voice sounds in the elbows of the hallways. We tuck our nerve endings under our collars, up our sleeves. Towers of folders balance tipsy on stacks of loose papers. Manuals heap on floors. A small copse of PR posters lean into the corner behind my door.

Now this third merger. We hold our breath. A new *Manual for Better Ways* arrives. It bears the new logo: a hand around a flower. More new policies, more new directors, more new approaches for delivering health and services, for saving money. The pace fiercer. Deadlines closer.

My briefcase splits along one side of the exterior pocket. Pencils, pens spring out. Values and determination clatter to the floor. Beliefs and paper clips rain from the side.

I dream about caymans and alligators. their mouths smile wide as bellows stocked with pin-point teeth. after 7 the building doors auto-lock, no one in and no one out. cellphones die mid-conversation. elevators stick between the screaming floors until the throats of passengers are dry. stragglers stranded overnight: the secretary who stays to finish agendas for the next day, three managers from planning working on a new strategic plan, the Quality Assurance team from a late meeting. they lick salt and vinegar chips from lunchroom vending machines, slug the on-tap coffee free-of-charge. vacant-eyed till 4 at window walls, their palms adhered like suction grips. found slumped at tables, on desks at 7 in the morning. smelling like vinegar.

I no longer even think beyond this building. my edgy razor view. the walls
of this building grow
inside my skull, inside my house, inside my car, inside my sleep.

I am pulling apart in two, slowly like bread dough. Stretching long. I can't tell how much dough is in the length of pull, the suspension of this yeasty weight, how much will break off into my hand to rise, how much dough will stay in the bank.

After his heart attack, my father returned to his office in Old Montreal. His smile had thinned but he still tried to joke with his stable of salesmen, eat smoked meat at Moishe's. Working part-time, he said, but soon his boss said part-time wouldn't do. Who wants a part-time workaholic around the office? His boss said think about retirement; not as useful with his grey voice and his suit jacket drooping from his caving shoulders as he was in his pushed-back fedora, winking, jingling change in his pants pocket. His boss took his nameplate from his door, called my mother, said: he's too sick, tell him to quit.

His face was caved, with smudgy crescents underlining pale blue eyes. He asked his boss about his pension. Too little, my father replied. In the end too little. But in the end they did not want him as partial. In the end he took his too-little pension and went home.

He stayed home. He shouted in the kitchen. He shouted at the counter and in his chair at the table. He banged the table with his balled-up hand. In the end my mother said: Tom, your heart.

He took up lawn bowling. He golfed. He read the newspaper to my mother. He shopped for discount frozen orange juice. He wore pastel trousers and pastel pork pie hats. He went to Florida in November. He did not know how or what else to be.

And my mother always: Relax Tom relax; remember your heart. But his heart wasn't in it. Or out of it. My father becoming smaller, needing his pastel pants taken in at the waist and new pastel T-shirts. His retirement telescoped before him. The wrong end of life.

When he stayed alone in the house, he could not sit down, he walked in and out of rooms. She had to bring him with her everywhere she went. He drove with her to the shopping centre, to the pharmacy, to the lawn bowling club. Wearing his golf shirt and his pork pie hat, his mouth pursed.

He had entered her territory. And found it was too small for him, his elbows always sticking out. He was never much at home before. He still jingled change in his pockets but his pockets were lighter. He still bought new cars but the cars were less expensive. He didn't rush around in the morning, he didn't nick his chin shaving, he didn't apply the membrane of a soft boiled egg. He didn't eat eggs anymore. He had to learn where she kept the pots and pans, how long to simmer oatmeal. It wasn't what he had expected, but who anticipates how things will end. In the end, her house was his only place, he had no more office to go to. Not working was a change, it was a rest, but for him it was not good.

My Director, Lana, slips into my office and shuts the door behind her. It's only 8:45. Monday morning.

Jim was severed this morning, she tells me, then turns to the window, stares at the razor wire on the concrete wall.

My lips form the question, which she anticipates, her shoulders lifting in unison with her pencilled eyebrows.

He got the full treatment, she continues, escorted from the building, took nothing with him. Jennifer, his admin assistant, she's gone too. All in 10 minutes. Poof! She snaps her hands like a magician.

That's it? We don't ever see him again?

She nods and nods, her head on a spring, bobbing, the rhythm soothing. Yep, yep. Along with five other VP's. All six. Gone, just like that. She lifts her shoulders and her eyebrows in unison.

We listen to the hum of the air-conditioning. Like we just heard that someone we know got hit by a bus, our faces hanging down.

How would you feel? she asks me a little pointedly. Outside, I notice, the wind whips a swirl of newspapers. They lift together like flying saucers.

You mean if . . . ?

I know you're thinking . . .

My mouth opens but stays silent, which surprises me, my mouth silent around my desire to escape. I fondle a yellow pencil, roll it round in my right palm, read the gold print on the side: Eagle HB. She waits, watching the razor wire, chewing at her mouth.

On balance, I say finally, sounding too deliberate, balancing the pencil on its eraser end, the lead point up. On balance, I'm . . . I think I'd be okay with it. I drop the pencil. It's not the way . . . I begin to explain. I stop myself, lean over to retrieve the pencil from the carpet. My door opens.

my mother died hard. years of Rothmans at the kitchen counter and her lungs turned black. my father died hard. years of Export A's in his office in his car and his breathing stopped. they both lead lives filled with the conventions of the times: smoking, selling, ironing shirts. neither had answers when they arrived at death. for them, it was just dying. they gave me an environment, they did not give me answers. they could not help me understand my world, though both had tried.

when my mother died I was released from worldly working aspirations, understanding that her life, though not of worldly consequence, had been a full life lived with kindness.

when my father died, history released me into unmediated blue, silver constellations ka-ching, ka-chinging, murmurous as bracelet bells.

then
on a high hill my face into the blast of future
the wind buffets and blows

no mother no father no work no house no one

between
me and limitless sky

I want to go home

It begins: "We regret to inform you that your services are no longer. . . ." I look up at Lana. She sits with her arms folded in front of her, leaning forward on the table. Looking almost relaxed, but her mouth stays tight. She can't make herself smile. We've worked together too long. She looks at her copy of the letter.

Read it through, she scoops her chin in my direction, in case you have any questions.

My eyes land in the middle of the first paragraph on a line that ends with "the severance of your employment with this organization." I keep pretending to read. It's six pages of legal jargon with three separate sheets for signatures. I flip through the pages but the words jump around, slip off my eyes. This should make me happy. My heart a ping pong.

Don't sign it till you've thought it through. She smooths her copy from the bottom up. Go home early. Talk to Cath about it. She smooths her skirt over her knees. Sleep on it.

As if sleep.

Why do I think now of Benedict Labre? That house in Montreal fluent with good works. A drab house inside with yellowed linoleum curling at splits around the edges, at the thresholds. And drab outside with dogs roaming curbsides grey with frozen rags splayed inside the pitted ice. A bleak row house bricked brown and storied. Managed by a saint who promised sandwiches and canned soup each day, simple, made by highschool girls with fumbly hands almost righteous and out of place. Their skidding smiles, lowered eyes, trying not to shame the threadbare woollen jackets brown and pulling across thin shouldered men, the men, with thanks and thanks and thanks, their faces red from January cold and sudden indoor heat. That awful smell of furnace oil mixed with tomato soup redolent in our highschool back-combed hair on the way home in the teacher's car along the 2 & 20 looking out the car's side windows into darkening banks of snow.

Why think of this now? Expect that half day of Wonderbread and rheumy eyes to give me any answers? The past, buried along some snow-packed highway. Past speaking now to now, having seen beyond schools and driveways shoveled bare, kitchen counters and industrial soaps, pearlized prayers where mouths move round and round and never an answer.

The world redolent with disappointment, too much canned soup and grey. Eyes still restless trying to fix on answers that mist down narrow halls, disappear and twist round bends, through doors at the end of corridors. As if answers are material. As if each story reconciles. As if the parts of story need to come together, point somewhere.

If I could say it made me sick and I wanted to be well. If I could say my heart was split and split again but I gather all the pieces. If I could say the answer's somewhere inside the splits, along the edges: the space between the parts is where to look. I pull pieces of me back into me, seeing every unsmooth edge. I live the spaces in between, wanting all the years, all the work, my mother and my father, written back together, trusting the magnetic field of ink can hold each piece of me beside the other.

Home and office, school and fire doors and hallways that stretch and bend for years, high-rise windows that never let in air, the blue dumpster in the lane, the thresholds, the chosen, and the ones denied, the boy who sold yellow pencils on St. Catherine St., the woman with the red bandana'd dog, the sidewalk wet beneath her broken square of cardboard, the homeless and the housed, the men who park imported cars in underground parkades, the sparrows in the spring, the menace of every 6 AM, and those who will not leave. I lived the gulf between my parents. Writing all the pieces of a working life onto the page. Each piece marked along a line. Loosely linked. Believing in the page.

Kafka once told me: inside the unscored space is the freedom that you crave; seek to unbelong. It is inevitable to want an end: a door closed brings more quiet. It is as simple as that, he said and faded.

At the elevator, the secretary with the yellow beads, waiting with a file box in her arms for the up elevator, asks me if I'm feeling sick, thinking that must be the reason I am leaving the building so early in the day with my briefcase overflowing.

Feeling fine, I tell her as I step into the down elevator and break suddenly into a grin so broad I can feel my face breaking. The doors close before I tell her much how I've counted on her yellow beads. Some kind of yellow amber. Like bees in a rock.

The doors slide closed, brushed-silver blank with a meeting in the middle. Then the short pause before the elevator descends.

I slam my car door, hoist my broken briefcase onto the passenger seat beside me and pens and yellow stick-em's cascade onto the seat. I ease out of #19, tight round the cement pillar, over the release cable just before the exit ramp.

The steel gate clanks open. More ponderous than usual, I think, reminded of moats and caymans. Nudge up the ramp as the gate lifts, and brake, in position for the gate's yawn to open wide enough for my car to squeeze under.

I enter the lane, miss the red side of a panel truck by inches, and nose into the thin stream of traffic on the side street. Wait. Is that Kafka at the crosswalk? I almost hit the car in front of me. Wind whisks his fedora and he swivels round before I can see his face. Traffic honking, stop-starting. Left turn at the light onto the bridge on-ramp, then gunning it, accelerator to the floor, flying now. Rolling down my window, hang my elbow out. The early springtime air breaks on my cheeks like chimes. Sunshine bounces like arc-welding off my hood, my windshield, scatters from the vertical joists of the bridge, zings off the high-rise panes across the inlet. Beyond are the North Shore mountains, which should be green today, but in fact are blue. I'm on my way home. Blue, I say out loud, those mountains really are.

ARLEEN PARÉ has graduate degrees in Social Work and Adult Education and is currently working on a degree in Creative Writing. Originally from Montreal, she worked for over two decades in Vancouver in Social Service bureaucracies. Paré now resides in Victoria, where she lives with her partner, Chris Fox. She has two adult sons.